Release the Stars

HARPER BLISS

Also by Harper Bliss

Once in a Lifetime
At the Water's Edge
French Kissing Season Two
French Kissing Season One
High Rise (The Complete Collection)

For Caroline, always my brightest star

CHAPTER ONE

"You're the toast of the town, sweetie," Nick said. "Every woman in this place wants a piece of you."

Charlie rolled her eyes at him. "Wrong bar. This isn't Lux." Her request to go to her favorite lesbian club had been ignored in favor of the newest, brightest, shiniest scene.

"Next time. I promise." Nick sipped his cosmo. "*This* is where it's at these days."

Charlie shook her head. She tried hard to not give in to the negative vibes Nick kept scolding her about and go with the flow—also Nick's advice. Charlie was convinced that spending some time at Lux could change that, but for reasons she couldn't understand, Nick was reluctant to go there. Maybe because he was gay. But why it mattered to him was beyond her. Nick was happily married to a man who was, objectively speaking, way too hot for him.

"I don't even know why you care," Charlie said with a sigh.

"This is LA, Charlie dear. Things are different here." He didn't look at her directly, but kept his gaze focused somewhere behind Charlie. He touched her arm. "Okay, don't look, but—"

Charlie interrupted by following his line of sight and looking straight at the face of a typical LA woman. It was as though women on the West Coast were a different species from the ones she was used to hanging around.

"Tsk. Now you've ruined it. She was giving you the eye." He swung his hands in the air dramatically. "Way to play it cool."

Nick was one of the most un-cool people living in WeHo.

"You should be out of practice," Charlie said. "What with having put a ring on the most gorgeous man in Los Angeles."

Charlie was severely out of practice as well, but she was pretty sure she wasn't going to find what she was looking for on the rooftop of the newest and hippest Sunset Strip hotel. There was a glass cage in the reception area with a model locked in it, for God's sake. Charlie assumed the woman went in voluntarily, but still.

"Are you Nick Kent?" A shrill voice came from behind Charlie. "You *are*," the voice shrieked. "Can I get a photo, please?"

When she stepped into view, it turned out to be the same woman Nick had pointed out earlier. Instead of checking *her* out, as Nick presumed, she'd had her eye on him. Charlie couldn't wait to throw that back into his face.

"In the flesh," he said, a huge smile on his face. Nick had one of the lead parts in a popular sitcom, so it was imperative that he appear jovial and courteous at all times when meeting fans. "My friend here will take it for us." He shot Charlie a quick wink.

The woman handed Charlie her phone and didn't give her a further glance. Charlie took the camera and renewed her determination to drag Nick away from this place. He'd gotten his fan-girl fix; someone had spotted and approached him at the new "it" bar. Now he could indulge his lesbian friend for the rest of the evening.

Charlie fulfilled her duty and snapped a photo of Nick and the woman as they pulled their lips into the obligatory duck-face pout. Charlie had been in Los

Angeles for six months now, but she still had some massive acclimatizing to do.

"Thank you so, so much," the woman said, fawning over Nick. "I adore you on *Laughing Matters*. You're my favorite character by far."

"Thank you," Nick said with a tilt of his head. "I won't tell the others." It took a few more seconds before the woman returned to her own party.

Charlie arched her eyebrows, hoping to convey a wordless *I told you so*.

"Okay, fine." Nick showed her his palms. "You've got this one. I was wrong. I'll go to Lux with you as penance. Too many out-of-towners here who don't know how to behave amongst the likes of me." He giggled self-consciously. One of the reasons why they got along so well was because he was one of the most self-deprecating people she knew. Plus they had a history in New York. She'd met him years ago, around the same time she'd met Jo.

"You're a star," Charlie said flatly.

"Tell me something I don't know," Nick replied and got up.

* * *

"It's like you're a different person here, Charlie. Just relax," Nick said.

But Charlie found it hard to relax with a dozen women staring at her, their gazes burning into the back and side of her head. "I need more booze." She looked around for a waiter.

"Erm, orders at the bar, dear," Nick said. "You know that."

"You get them." Charlie couldn't bear the thought of making her way through the throng of women blocking her path to the bar. Not because they were unattractive, or too LA for her taste. Rather, she was intimidated. That word summed up the last six months of her life quite adequately. Los Angeles was too shiny on the outside, its inhabitants too focused on appearance. Everything and everyone looked polished and slick. Back when Charlie was an anonymous novelist in New York, she'd never felt like this, so out of her depth.

"Oh no, I got the first round." Nick gave her a smug smile. "And you wanted to come here. Don't tell me you're too chicken to order." He shrugged nonchalantly. "God forbid you'd have to talk to an actual lesbian on the way. I mean, for someone with your aspirations, this place must embody your wildest dreams come true." He leaned over their table. "One hundred percent lesbian, Charlotte, my darling. Your exact words. So what's the problem? This place is teeming with exactly the kind of woman you're looking for."

"Screw you, Nick Kent," Charlie said because she didn't know what else to say. "Same again?"

"Yes, please." He threw back the last of his cosmopolitan and leaned luxuriously against the backrest of his chair, ready to be waited on.

Charlie wanted to say "Nobody even drinks cosmos anymore," but that would just be mean. Nick didn't deserve that. Plus, he might take her comment too seriously.

So, Charlie made her way to the bar. The earth did not shatter, and she was not attacked by a pack of glossy LA lesbians. The customers standing around the bar even gave her enough room to speak to the bartender. In addition to Nick's frou-frou drink, she ordered a margarita—an evergreen cocktail that would never go out of style—for herself.

"Aren't you here with Nick Kent?" a short man with a receding hairline asked. It was just Charlie's luck to be addressed by the only other man in the bar.

"Just someone who looks like him," she said, but Nick was so recognizable with his ginger beard, it was futile. She'd gotten used to people recognizing Nick when they were out together, but Lux wasn't the kind of place where she expected that to happen. The typical customer here was too cool to bother. So, Charlie smiled at the man to let him know she was joking.

"I don't want to disturb him," the man said. "I was just wondering, you know?"

"Sure." Charlie checked out the bartender. She was dressed in a tight, black tank top, which displayed an elaborate tattoo snaking from her arm up to her shoulder. Quite possibly one hundred percent lesbian, she concluded.

"Aren't you…" the man paused to reflect, "that hot-shot writer working on that new show everyone in town is talking about?"

Charlie chuckled. She was *only* a writer. LA was littered with the anonymous almost-but-not-quite famous like her. Sure, the rights to her *Underground* book series had caused a bidding war among the studios two years ago, and her face had appeared in a few trade periodicals since then. But that didn't mean a whole lot in a city where everybody was *somebody*.

"I wouldn't say hot-shot," Charlie replied.

"I so can't wait for that show to air," the man said, getting excited.

"Here you go." The bartender placed two cocktails on the counter. "That'll be thirty."

Charlie dug some bills out of her wallet, scooped up the two glasses, shot the man an apologetic smile, and headed back to Nick.

"Enjoy," he shouted after her.

"At least I met a one hundred percent-gay *man*." She deposited their drinks on the table. "Progress, right?"

"I saw." Nick chuckled. "What can I say, Charlie?

The gays adore you. It must be that androgynous thing you have going on."

Charlie took a few big gulps from her margarita and looked around the bar. A few more of these and she'd be anyone's. Her reverie was interrupted by the sound of a message arriving on Nick's phone. When Nick's husband, Jason, was out of town, they had the habit of texting back and forth like middle schoolers.

"What sort of sweet nothing is Jason digitally whispering in your ear now, Nickie?"

"It's not from Jason." Nick's facial expression lost some of its usual playfulness.

"Oh." Charlie didn't know if she should inquire further.

"It's from Jo."

"Oh," Charlie repeated, but in an entirely different tone. "What does that bitch want?" It came out a bit harsher than she had intended, but the alcohol was not missing its effect, and, well, Jo had treated her in a manner that warranted a little bitchiness on Charlie's part.

"She's asking how you're doing since you don't reply to any of her e-mails or texts." He gave her a disapproving look. "She's worried about you."

"You can tell her I'm at a lesbian bar surrounded by women who are fully secure in their sexuality and who don't go back to men at the first sign of trouble."

"Now now," Nick said. "Let's at least try to be fair."

"Please don't pick her side again, Nick. She left me for a *man*. I deserve your sympathy here."

"I have shown you the utmost sympathy, sweetie. I've welcomed you into my adopted city with open arms. I've shown you around. Taken away that first sting of loneliness. I've basically become your best friend, so no need to lecture me on sympathy."

The alcohol made Charlie more forthright than she would normally be. "She now shares a bed with Christian

Robson." Apparently three margaritas hadn't numbed all of Charlie's pain, because it shot through her as if Jo had only broken up with her the week before, as opposed to months ago when it had actually happened.

"That's a fact," Nick said. "But, as you and I both know, because we are both reasonable adults, there are always two sides to every story."

"Oh, stop playing devil's advocate, already." A weight settled in Charlie's stomach, a weight she'd tried to outrun by moving west and taking up a writer's position in Hollywood, working on the TV show based on her most successful books. Something she would never have done if Jo hadn't broken up with her.

"It's been almost a year, Charlie. It's time to move on and to stop holding grudges. You're only hurting yourself. Jo simply wants to know if you've settled in okay and how this town is treating you."

Charlie pushed her half-full glass of margarita to the side. She'd had enough. "This… was not how it was supposed to go, Nickie. Me alone in this city full of fakes and wannabes. We had a good life in New York." *Until Jo blew it.*

"I moved here, too, sweetie. I know better than anyone that the transition can be hard. But you have me. You're not alone. And you're working on the hottest show Hollywood has seen in decades." Nick apparently wasn't done with his cosmo, nor with his speech. "And self-pity is so unattractive."

"It's easy for you to say. You have Jason. You are adored by millions. You're even friends with Ava Castaneda, for crying out loud." Ava Castaneda was the goddess who hosted the popular cooking show *Knives Out*. Charlie'd had a TV crush on her for years.

"I was wondering when you would bring Ava up today." Nick grinned at her. "I could introduce you, you know? Maybe that would cheer you up."

Charlie just waved him off. "I'm sorry for becoming such shit company. Hearing about Jo still rubs me the wrong way."

"I know, but look around you. Don't tell me that, just because you and your ex-girlfriend broke up nine months ago, there's no one here you could potentially be interested in. I declare the grieving period officially over here and now."

Charlie wasn't sure she'd ever be done grieving the loss of Jo Cook. Perhaps she wasn't the easiest person to live with, but Jo had stayed with her for seven years, giving the impression that Charlie wasn't too bad after all, only to do a runner when Charlie had least seen it coming. And with a man. No matter how hard she tried, Charlie couldn't get over that fact.

"I'm drunk, Nickie," Charlie said. "I think I'm ready to hit the hay."

"You lesbians are supposed to drink us under the table." Nick emptied his drink, then reached for Charlie's glass. "You're such a lightweight, Char. I thought I trained you better." He chugged the rest of Charlie's margarita. "Come on. I'll take you home."

Home, Charlie thought, where nobody waits for me. She nodded and followed Nick out of the bar.

CHAPTER TWO

"We could use an extra player on our softball team," Liz said.

They were the only two people left in the writers' room. Everyone else had gone for a smoke or a coffee.

"You could do the bar scene, of course, if that's more your style," Liz continued, "but for lesbians, joining a softball team is *the* best way to meet 'like-minded' women."

Of course, Liz was a married woman herself. Instead of holding that against her, however, Charlie thought she should see it as an example of how things *could* work out in Los Angeles. "I don't know. I've never played before."

"That doesn't matter. You're American. It's basically in your DNA. You could just come and watch the first time. Have a beer on the sideline. Meet the girls."

Meet the girls. Charlie didn't know why, since arriving here—and since the brutal breakup with Jo—these words scared the hell out of her. She didn't use to be like this. But being dumped had shattered a great deal of her confidence, and there was also the minor issue of being severely out of practice when it came to chatting up women.

"We have a training session tonight. Why don't you join Sarah and me for a quick bite, and then we'll go together?" Liz locked her gaze on Charlie's, making it pretty clear saying no was not an option. "We're a really fun bunch, even if I do say so myself."

"Okay." Charlie acquiesced. "I'm in. But tonight I'll just be watching."

"Excellent." Liz held up her hand for a high five. Nobody ever high fived in New York. "Besides, I want you to meet someone."

"What?" Inwardly, she told herself to relax. But she'd been telling herself that since the day she'd arrived in LA. It hadn't worked thus far.

"Just kidding." Liz shot her one of her goofiest smiles. "I think I know what you're like by now. A writers' room is a pretty intimate environment."

"Tell me about it." Charlie had worked alone in a quiet office for the better part of her writing career. It was her natural habitat—one she missed terribly. Stepping into a writers' room for the first time had been an extremely stressful enterprise, and it had taken a few weeks before she'd gotten used to the interaction and the energy of working with fellow writers on a TV show. As far as stepping out of her comfort zone went, Charlie believed she'd done plenty of that already, what with moving west and changing her day-to-day life so drastically.

"Have I told you lately that this show is going to be awesome? I was so stoked to get hired for this. You have no idea."

Charlie had more than an idea. From the very beginning, Liz had come out as her biggest fan. Good thing she had a wicked sense of humor and made Charlie laugh—a highly needed activity—on a daily basis, otherwise Charlie might have had to quit working on the show altogether.

When she initially met with her agent and some studio executives to discuss the TV rights to *Underground*—with Jo still firmly by her side—it was the endless fawning that had irritated her most. Not because she was averse to praise, but because, coming from a certain type of person, it sounded insincere. She knew when a person was going through the motions, putting on a show meant to charm her. Charlie was allergic to that giggly, high-pitched tone of voice even the most robust men adopted when trying to slither their way into a signed contract with her.

"Don't stop now, Liz." Charlie had started to think of Liz as another good friend in Tinseltown. "Tell me more."

"I really want to show you off to my softball buddies. My popularity has grown exponentially since I started working on this show."

"Okay. Okay. Enough." Charlie evaluated Liz, who had big, round eyes and *always* wore a blazer.

"Thank goodness. I need to use the ladies' room before we continue."

Charlie walked out with Liz, leaned against a wall, and checked her phone. Nick had posted a picture of him and his dog, Annie, on Instagram, and Charlie clicked *like*. The next picture in her stream was one posted by Ava Castaneda. Unfortunately, the ultra-sexy TV host hadn't posted a picture of herself, but of a plate of food she'd cooked. Charlie liked that one as well.

She scrolled through the rest of her feed, before sending a text message to Nick.

I'm playing softball with a bunch of lesbians in WeHo tonight. Want to come?

Charlie sent it more as a joke than anything else. She could easily predict Nick's reply, which came within the next minute.

Hell no, girl. Have fun. xo

* * *

And Charlie did have fun. Over dinner with Liz and her wife, Sarah, she'd happily accepted two beers, while the others refrained, taking their upcoming practice session very seriously. By the time they arrived at the ball field, Charlie was enjoying a mild buzz that kept her mellow.

Liz introduced her to the team members, who were all very friendly—but not too friendly in the way that Charlie loathed so much. While they warmed up, Charlie sat next to a variety of women as they rotated through the game.

The sun hung low in the sky, and someone had brought a cooler with more beer, and when Charlie tilted her head back to drink, and the sun shed its evening rays on her face, she experienced something that a lesser person, one without Charlie's acute experience with disappointment, might describe as happiness. Charlie, however, was not the least bit open to that idea.

Still, she had to admit, the weather in Los Angeles was always good. The sun always showed up, and never in that muggy east-coast-summer kind of way that made you long for air-conditioned rooms and winter.

Charlie made small talk with most of the women; the depth of the conversation depended entirely on how long the person remained seated next to her.

"What do you think?" Liz asked when it was her turn on the bench. "Shall I order you a uniform?"

"I might be tempted." Charlie stared straight ahead. A woman who had introduced herself as Britt earlier missed an easy ball. "I'll need some practice, though."

"I'm not saying we—and by *we* I mean *I*—are not competitive, but we mainly do this for fun. Whether you can actually pitch or bat doesn't really matter. Britt over there couldn't hit a ball if it were about to smash her in the face, which it has, on numerous occasions."

Charlie laughed. "How often do you practice?"

"Once a week on Wednesdays, and then we have a league game on the weekend. Usually on Sunday morning."

"There's a league?"

"Of course there is. Our baby, Sharon, tends to show up hungover almost every Sunday, but the rest of us are pretty well-behaved. We have cats to put to bed and all that."

"At the risk of sounding terribly cliché, I've been thinking about getting a cat. I had two back in New York, but my ex got custody when we split. They live with a man now." Charlie couldn't help the bitterness coming from her mouth.

"Poor pussies," Liz said. Charlie had told her all about her messy, painful breakup a few times already.

"I want to be sure I'll be sticking around first. I don't want to say goodbye to another pet."

"Liz, you're up." Britt approached the bench. "I've had about enough, anyway." She crashed down next to Charlie. "Hand me a beer, will you?"

Charlie reached into the cooler and grabbed one for herself as well.

"Cheers," Britt said, then followed up with a sly grin. "Come here often? For the record, I know that pick-up line never works."

Charlie was too tipsy to get worked up about the mention of a pick-up line. Instead, she smiled back. "It's my first time," she said. "I guess that makes me a virgin."

Britt elbowed her in the bicep gently. "I'm not supposed to say, but some of the girls have a bet out on you."

"Excuse me?"

"Tiff, Josie, and Andrea over there, or The Terrible Three as we like to call them. Just ignore them, though. They're troublemakers."

"What sort of bet?" Charlie took a few more sips of beer, wondering what her life would be like without alcohol. Perhaps she'd never leave the house at all.

"Let me put it this way—after this game is done, you can expect some major hitting-on-you to commence."

"Oh Christ," Charlie muttered. "You're not serious, are you?"

"Well, you're single, hot, and you have a steady job. You're a catch, so…" Britt pulled up her shoulders.

"Who did you bet on?" Charlie asked.

"Oh, I would never." Britt played coy. "Actually, I bet on none of them—that was the fourth choice. You don't look like the kind of girl who can be easily picked up on the sidelines of a softball game. I might be wrong, but that's the impression I get."

"How about you?" Charlie looked at Britt sideways. A softball outfit never really looked flattering on anyone, but Britt seemed to fill hers out nicely. "Does anyone have any bets out on you?"

"Me? Why would they?"

"Don't know." Charlie shrugged. "'Cause you're kinda hot?" If this could be called flirting, she wasn't doing the best job.

Britt's laugh came all the way from the bottom of her belly. "I'm sorry," she said after her laughter subsided. "I wasn't expecting that at all."

"Come on, Britney," Andrea of the Terrible Three shouted. "One more round for you."

"I'm drinking already," Britt said, lifting up her can of beer as evidence. "And my name is Britt, with two Ts so less intelligent people like yourself know where it ends."

"You can't hear the second T, Britt." Andrea drew out the Ts. "I'll finish your beer."

"Fine." Britt got up. "But just so you don't waste

your breath, I told Charlie about the bet." With that, Britt ran onto the field. Charlie thought she detected a spring in her step that hadn't been there earlier.

"To clear up any misunderstanding," Andrea said, "Tiff, Josie, and I are not disrespectful women with only one thing on our mind. It was only a bit of a joke between us. I hope you're not offended."

"Of course not." Charlie emptied her third can of beer. The mild buzz she'd walked onto the field with had transformed into severe giddiness. "If anything, I'm flattered."

"Are you coming for a drink with us after? We go to a bar around the corner. You live in WeHo, right?"

If Andrea was even the tiniest bit of a player, the way she was rambling masked it expertly. Or maybe it was part of her game. Charlie just enjoyed the attention. Liz had been right. Attending a softball game was much more effective than bar crawling.

"Sure. I'd love to." Charlie smiled widely at Andrea just to toy with her a bit.

"I'm sure you get this a lot, but your novel *Crying Rivers* meant so much to me when it came out. I re-read it every year."

"Thank y—" Charlie started to say, but was cut off as the rest of the team rushed off the field. It looked as though practice had ended.

Half of the players high fived each other, while the other half didn't seem too bothered by the goings-on.

"Drinks are on you, losers," Josie said to the group of women huddled around Liz.

Of the Terrible Three, Charlie thought Josie to be most her type. She was Asian-American and had the sharpest cheekbones Charlie had seen in LA, and this being LA, she had seen quite a few.

"Charlie is joining us for drinks," Andrea said to Liz.

"Awesome. Let's go, lesbos," Liz said.

In New York, Charlie had hung out with a group of lesbians occasionally, but the vibe among them had been completely different than the one she got from this group of women at night fall. For all the shows it put on and its immediate fakeness, LA offered much more breathing room than New York. The canyons here were nature-made, as opposed to being a valley between two blocks of high-rise buildings.

At the bar, Charlie got involved in a long conversation with Andrea. Still, as her level of drunkenness increased, it became harder and harder to keep her eyes off Josie. While Andrea visited the washroom, Charlie quickly pulled Liz to the side and asked, "On a scale of one to a hundred, how lesbian is Josie?"

"Josie, huh?" Liz said, pulling her lips into a pout. "Is that the kind of woman you go for?" She pouted even more. "She's a lovely girl, really, but I've never really seen her with anyone longer than a few months. But, to answer your question, I think I can safely say she's a ninety-nine."

"What about the other one percent?" Charlie slurred her words.

"Nobody is a hundred percent, Charlie. We don't live in that kind of dreamworld." Liz slapped her on the shoulder as if she'd made a big joke. Charlie failed to get it, although she could, somewhere in the depths of her intoxicated mind, guess that Liz was ridiculing her percentage system.

"Look, Liz, I'm going to get out of here. I had a bit too much, and we have a big day tomorrow at work."

"You betcha," Liz said. "I do hope we can get Elisa. How super freaking awesome would that be?"

"It would be out of this world. Let's sleep with our fingers crossed." Charlie drew Liz into a hug. "Thanks for inviting me. I had fun." Charlie said her goodbyes to the rest of the team, ignoring the look of disappointment on Andrea's face, and lingering in Josie's space perhaps a bit longer than necessary for the exchange of a farewell.

She walked home in a bit of a zig-zag line, and further pondered what a coup it would be for *Underground* to bag Elisa Fox in its lead role. Then her thought process was rudely interrupted by the chime of her phone with a message from Nick.

How was muffball practice?

Charlie was wasted enough to ignore his comment. She texted back that she'd had fun. By the time she reached her house, she received another text from Nick.

Not as much fun as you're going to have this Saturday when you'll be my date at Ava Castaneda's dinner party.

Charlie's mouth fell open. What was he talking about? Another text quickly followed.

You can stop drooling now. Jason can't make it and you're the next best thing. Go shopping for something fancy.

CHAPTER THREE

"You're really not playing the cruelest prank in the world on me?" Charlie asked for the umpteenth time.

Nick's car service had picked her up in a town car, with Nick already in the backseat.

"Charlotte Cross, please listen to me. Not even I could be so coldhearted as to trick you into believing you're going to meet the woman you've been lusting after for years. I do have standards. I don't mess with people's crushes like that."

"I'm so nervous." Charlie squeezed Nick's knee between her restless fingers.

"It's just a casual dinner. Relax. She's the most divine cook. It's going to be wonderful."

"Who else is going to be there?"

Nick sighed. "I told you. I don't know."

"Does she know I'm coming and not Jason?"

"Yes." Nick put a hand on hers. "She's looking forward to having you, but Char... just one tiny word of advice."

"Yeah?"

"When you've had a few, you have a slight tendency to start going on about," he curled his fingers into air quotes, "'one hundred percent lesbians.' If you could save that for another night, that would be great."

Charlie was momentarily lost for words. "I don't really go on about that so much?" she said in a small voice.

"When you have some booze in you and your filters, erm, stop filtering the way they should. I'm saying this as a friend, okay? Please don't take offense."

"I won't." Charlie was definitely offended. More than that, she was embarrassed. She racked her memory for times when she'd mentioned the subject. There were one or two nights that she could remember bringing up how she would never date a woman again who didn't have a proven track record of being a lesbian. Not that she would go exclusively for gold stars, but she had to do something, even if it was ridiculous. She couldn't handle another breakup like the one from Jo.

The car wound its way up the coastal highway toward Malibu, where Ava's house was located.

"You've gone all quiet." Nick said it in the voice his TV alter ego often employed to get something he wanted. "That really wasn't my intention. Come back to me, my friend, please come back."

Charlie waved him off, straightened her spine, and focused on the fact that within fifteen minutes she'd come face-to-face with Ava Castaneda. The gorgeous Latina wasn't only a former model, she'd also hosted the same popular cooking show *Knives Out* for the past fifteen years. An impressive feat in the current TV landscape. Charlie wasn't much of a cook herself, but she was a loyal viewer nonetheless because she needed her weekly dose of ogling the tall brunette.

"How did you meet her again?" Charlie asked as the car pulled up to an impressive driveway leading up to a high fence.

"Nick Kent and company," the driver said into the intercom, and the gates swung open.

"I'm gay and famous, darling. Everyone wants to be my friend, especially the mega-gorgeous." He leaned over and whispered in her ear, "That includes you, by the way."

Charlie knew he said it to give her a confidence boost.

A few moments later, they stood in front of Ava's surprisingly modest house. It wasn't a small, humble abode by a long shot, but it wasn't the mansion Charlie had expected either.

"Nickie!" Ava walked out of the front door, arms open wide. She wore a long, off-white dress that highlighted the bronze color of her skin sublimely.

Charlie hadn't even said hello and she was already trying to catch her breath.

"Hello, beautiful." Nick threw his arms around Ava. Charlie waited silently. It was a real hug between friends, not one of those halfhearted Hollywood embraces she'd experienced too often since moving to LA.

"And you must be Charlotte," Ava said after she and Nick broke away from each other. Charlie had expected an outstretched arm for a handshake, but instead Ava pulled her into a hug as well. "Welcome to my home."

"It's an honor to be here," Charlie mumbled. "Please, call me Charlie. Even my own mother hasn't called me Charlotte since I was ten." Because of the nerves running amok in her system, Charlie was unable to enjoy the warmth of Ava's embrace. She curved her arms delicately around Ava's shoulders, as though Ava was made of the most breakable porcelain. "I am such a big fan of yours." Charlie had heard the same words tossed around far too often in this town, so they sounded a bit trite, even though she meant them with all her heart.

"And I of you. I heard about Elisa Fox joining your show. That's quite something."

"It sure is," Nick chimed in.

Ava rested her gaze on Charlie for a few more seconds. It was as though Ava glowed under the fading evening light. Charlie had never seen anyone as beautiful in person before. Ava's dark brown eyes seemed to look straight into her heart—a ridiculous and unsettling sensation.

"Do come in." Ava led the way inside and then outside again to a back patio overlooking the ocean. "The other guests have arrived already."

Ava's house was appointed stylishly, but not lavishly. Unlike the size of the house, this was exactly what Charlie had expected. The view of the ocean, however, was nothing short of astounding.

"Nick, you've met Eric and Sandra before." They rose and beamed smiles at Nick and Charlie. Charlie recognized Eric as the head judge of *Knives Out* and, if the specialized press was to be believed, Ava's on-and-off boyfriend.

Eric, Nick, and Sandra hugged, then Ava introduced them to Charlie.

"Sandra's my publicist, and you might recognize this gentleman."

"I most certainly do." Charlie exchanged quick cheek kisses with these people she didn't know, then tried to figure out if, perhaps, Eric and Sandra were an item.

After they'd all sat down, Ava poured Cristal from a bottle she kept in a fifties-style ice bucket next to her chair.

"Thank you all for coming." Ava made a point of clinking her glass against all four of theirs and making eye-contact while doing so. A part of Charlie melted when it was her turn. Every other woman she'd ever been vaguely interested in, and even the ones she'd had actual relationships with, faded in comparison to the gorgeous woman sitting across from her.

That didn't take very long, a mocking voice inside her head said. *Five minutes in her company and you're smitten like a teenager.* Charlie couldn't argue. She didn't want to either. She just wanted to appreciate the elegant way Ava disposed of the bottle and crossed her legs to reveal a bit of smooth thigh through the split in her dress.

Nick had nothing to worry about. Ghosts of her past were very unlikely to haunt her tonight—Jo Cook was all but forgotten. Charlie was perfectly content just reveling in Ava's grace and beauty.

"How do you like Hollywood?" Ava asked, later, when they sat at the outside dining table. Ava had insisted that Charlie sit facing the ocean. The splendor of Ava Castaneda against the backdrop of the sun setting over the Pacific affected Charlie so deeply she could barely swallow her food.

"It's... interesting," Charlie said.

"If you ever need a publicist," Sandra interjected, "I'm your woman." She was pleasant enough. She and Eric hadn't displayed any signs of being involved with each other. Nor had Ava and Eric, for that matter. Perhaps, for once, Charlie wasn't the only single person at the party.

"I've read all the *Underground* books," Ava said. "I can't wait to see what it will look like on TV."

This took Charlie aback. "You have?"

"Of course. Any book about an all-female, ass-kicking, clandestine spy agency is right up my alley." Ava fixed Charlie with that look again. "I wasn't lying when I said I'm a fan. In fact—and no offense to your lovely husband, Nickie—I was delighted when Nick asked if he could bring you tonight instead of Jason."

"Please, Ava, stop. This one will be unbearable on the way home," Nick said.

"Are they changing the sexual preference of Aretha from lesbian to straight like Hollywood execs love to do?" Sandra asked.

"Absolutely not." Charlie shifted position in her chair. "I made it clear from the very beginning of negotiations that no one would get the rights if they had

23

that intention."

"Hear! Hear!" Nick faux-clapped his fingertips together. "More gays and lesbians on TV!"

"And this is cable, so you know, the limits to what we can show are not as constrained." Charlie remembered the scene they had constructed in the writers' room the day before, of the chief spy Aretha questioning a person of interest in a very *interesting* manner.

"I literally want to bounce up and down in my seat right now. That's how excited I am." Ava looked deep into Charlie's eyes again, and this time, with quite a few glasses of champagne and wine swirling in her blood, Charlie couldn't keep from blushing when Ava asked, "When is the premiere?"

"I'm not sure I'm allowed to say yet. The network hasn't released that information."

"Oh, come on." Ava snaked her hand across the table and put it on Charlie's. "Your secret is definitely safe here."

Charlie couldn't look away from Ava's hand cradling hers. She would never be able to wash that particular patch of skin ever again. Ava only let her hand linger briefly, but she was clearly a tactile person who expressed her emotions—and impatience—through lots of hand gestures. Charlie was wise enough not to look for a deeper meaning behind it, but the fire that had been lit when Ava threw her arms around her earlier, flared even higher.

"Okay, well, if you all pledge to not repeat what I'm about to say…" She glanced around the table. Eric looked a bit absentminded, as though not very interested in the TV show Charlie was working on, while Ava and Sandra looked quite excited about it.

"My word is my bond." Ava presented two out-stretched fingers.

"I'm a publicist. My job is basically keeping other people's secrets. Usually far dirtier than the premiere date of a much-hyped show. So yes, of course, you have my word," Sandra said.

"Yes, yes," Nick said. "Someone on the crew is going to leak this soon, anyway. Just get on with it. No need to make such a fuss."

Charlie shot him a stern look before speaking. "Negotiations with Elisa have been on-going, and we had a back-up in case she pulled out last minute, so we start shooting the week after next." Charlie wanted to follow Ava's example and bounce up and down for a while at the prospect of seeing her words come to life on screen. "The premiere date is approximately seven months from now on Sunday, January seventeenth.

"No." Ava groaned. "Do I really have to wait that long?"

"I think we all know patience is not even considered a virtue in this town. It's more a bare necessity," Eric said.

"Speaking of," Ava said, "I won't keep you in suspense about the main course any longer." She got up and headed for the kitchen.

"Do you need a hand?" Sandra asked.

"No. All my guests ever have to do when they come here is relax," Ava shouted from the doorway.

The starter had been scallop ceviche, and Charlie was curious as to what Ava had concocted for the main, but she could hardly claim she was hungry. Tipsy, yes. Mesmerized by Ava, for sure. Her stomach was in tatters.

Ava came out of the house carrying the entrée of lamb tagine, and despite her lack of appetite, Charlie finished it to the last morsel. She'd rather face an uncomfortable feeling in her stomach than be impolite by not eating Ava's food.

"Actually, I may need a hand with bringing out

dessert." Ava looked at Charlie as though she were the only other person at the table. Sandra had gone to wash her hands and Eric and Nick were deep into a discussion about which talent agency was better—TPA or Berkovitz. Charlie had been staring at the sea, floating on a cloud of contentment because of her environment, the delicious food, and the more-than-exquisite company.

"Of course." She shot out of her chair, her legs numb from sitting too long in the same position, and followed Ava into the kitchen. She'd cast a glance inside earlier on her way to the bathroom, but now that she had the time to properly observe the room, she was blown away by the restaurant-grade kitchen tools and equipment.

"The kitchen is the most important room in my house," Ava said, obviously noticing Charlie's bewilderment at how elaborately her kitchen was outfitted.

"I can assure you it's the least important one in mine," Charlie blurted out, not really realizing what she was saying. After all, she was alone in a room with Ava. Her brain refused to function under the circumstances.

"Maybe we should try and change that someday," Ava said with a mischievous smile on her face. "I can teach you some basics if that's what you're after."

What am I after? Charlie had no idea, but if Ava was offering to spend time with her, she would gladly take it. For now, all she could do was chuckle self-consciously.

Ava rummaged in the freezer and unearthed a container of ice cream. "Homemade, of course." She lifted the lid, and even though Charlie was not very hungry, she couldn't wait to taste it. "I'm going to put dollops of this in hot coffee, so they'll need to go out fast. That's why I asked you to help."

"Of course. At your service." Charlie tried to lean against a cabinet nonchalantly. She suspected she was failing miserably. But Ava must be used to silly admirers like Charlie, so, instead of worrying about how she came across, she focused on how swiftly and methodically Ava worked. A few minutes later the first two desserts were ready to go, and Charlie did her best not to trip on the way out.

When she returned, Sandra was in the kitchen with Ava. "I've got these, darling," she said. "Do sit back down."

The sun had completely set by now, and the ocean was a dark mass against the night sky. Charlie tried to imagine Ava coming out here in the morning in her robe, enjoying a cup of coffee before starting her day. Perhaps the side of her robe would slip off and display some of the lusciously smooth—

"Here you go." Ava planted an affogato in front of Charlie. "Enjoy. As of now, it's my time to fully relax."

"I thought feeding your friends scrumptious dishes *was* your way of relaxing," Nick said.

"It is." Ava took a bit of ice cream and then licked her spoon in a way Charlie wouldn't be able to forget any time soon. "But I'm a woman in my mid forties, and I do get tired after dark these days."

How refreshing, Charlie thought. A working woman in Hollywood who wasn't ashamed to admit she was over forty. Throughout the evening, Ava had impressed her time and again.

After an elaborate goodbye involving hugs and cheek kisses, Charlie found herself in the backseat of Nick's car again.

"And they say you should never meet your heroes," she mused. "They—whoever 'they' are—are so very wrong."

"How's that crush of yours evolving, Charlie?" Nick asked. "Not going away anytime soon, I take it?"

"I didn't even know people like her exist in real life.

I have to revise my position on make-believe in this town." Charlie sighed. "She's perfect. She has zero faults, making the rest of us look like frumpy, unaccomplished wannabes at life."

"Speak for yourself." Nick playfully punched her in the arm. "I consider myself fairly accomplished."

There were so many things Charlie could say, but she didn't have the energy for it. All the vigor she had left in her for the day went to conjuring up the image of Ava licking a dessert spoon.

CHAPTER FOUR

"Do we really need to go to this thing?" Charlie asked Liz. The network had sent a car for them, and they were cruising over Mulholland Drive, up to one of the most lavish mansions in the hills.

"*You* don't. You're Charlie Cross. You're basically going to make this guy a shitload of money. However, I do." Liz patted Charlie on the knee. "Thank you for helping me suck up to my employer, buddy." Liz batted her eyelashes. "You can ask me for anything you want in return."

"You introduced me to the great sport of softball. So I actually owe you." Charlie looked at Liz. She had one of the friendliest faces she'd encountered in LA, and Charlie was lucky to count her among the few friends she had here.

"I'm not a big fan of schmooze fests like this either, but I'm just over the moon I actually get to go." Liz's voice was growing more excited. Abe Eisenberg, the CEO of EBC was having a big shindig to celebrate his fiftieth birthday and had invited half of Hollywood.

The car took a few turns then came to a stop. "Get your smile on, Lizzie." Charlie exited the car through the passenger door which had been opened from the outside for them.

"Wowzers," Liz said. She was wearing her super fancy blazer for the occasion.

"I know." Charlie took in the magnificently lit up

house in front of her. Jo would have loved being her plus-one for this because she'd be allowed to wander freely and investigate the work of a top-notch interior designer. "This is just obscene."

A man dressed in a tuxedo escorted them inside, where the party seemed to be in full swing already.

"Let's see who we know." Liz scanned the living room.

Charlie glanced around. This room was at least twice as big as the spacious loft she'd shared with Jo in New York.

"There's Michelle." Liz jabbed Charlie in the arm. "Let's go say hello to our esteemed showrunner."

On the way over, they were offered champagne and Charlie drank greedily. It was strange to be invited to the birthday party—and his fiftieth no less—of a man she barely knew. She'd met Eisenberg a few times, but he'd invited the entire writing staff of *Underground* and probably every other EBC show.

"I hear he'll be having five parties," Michelle said. "This is the first one. The warm-up, I guess."

"It's so nice of him to invite us here. This place is crazy," Liz said. Her wide eyes grew even wider as she gazed around the room again. For the most part, the furniture was white with a few dashes of turquoise and darker blue as accents.

"Have you been outside?" Michelle asked. "I think a hundred people can swim in that pool simultaneously."

"We must go check that out." Liz finished her champagne and, as if by magic, was immediately offered another. "Are you coming, Charlie?"

Charlie drained her glass and happily accepted a fresh one. They made their way through a throng of people Charlie had never seen before. On the other side of the living room, glass doors had been slid open and the inside of the house seamlessly transitioned into the outside to reveal a lush, elegantly lit garden with a huge pool and a spectacular view over the city.

"Jesus," Charlie whispered.

"Elisa Fox probably lives in a crib like this," Liz said. "If we play our cards right, we might get invited."

"Charlie?" a voice Charlie didn't immediately recognize, said her name. "Sandra, remember?" Sandra, Ava Castaneda's friend and agent, took her by the shoulders and pecked Charlie very lightly on the cheeks.

Of course Charlie remembered. Every little detail of last Saturday was etched in her memory forever. Charlie introduced Sandra to Liz and they exchanged a few pleasantries.

"Abe and I—" Sandra started to say, but was interrupted by a voice Charlie *would* easily recognize out of a million.

"Charlie!" Ava said and, in true Hollywood fashion, threw her arms around Charlie as though they'd been friends forever instead of having shared one meal together. Not that Charlie minded in the least. Ava's hug was far too brief for her liking. Though the evening was looking up—greatly.

After introducing Ava to Liz, Charlie asked her, "How come you're invited to the D-list party?"

"Oh, I wasn't even invited," Ava said. "I came as Sandra's plus-one." Ava didn't seem to mind this fact in the slightest and shot Charlie a big grin. She was dressed in an informal orange dress that made the amber flecks in her eyes stand out. The slim straps of the dress accentuated Ava's square shoulder line in a way that made Charlie salivate.

"Ladies and gentlemen, may I have your attention, please?" a voice announced over the sound system. "The entertainment has arrived."

The soft lounge music that had been playing was replaced by a Bollywood tune and a dozen dancers clad in brightly colored robes emerged from the dark recesses of the garden.

"Oh yes," Ava shouted over the music. "I love this." Her hips started swaying to the beat.

Everyone gathered on the patio between the house and the swimming pool and looked on as the dancers performed a very intricate dance.

"How about you, Charlie?" Ava whispered in her ear. "Do you like to dance?"

Charlie was standing between Ava and Liz and their body heat radiated onto her skin. Charlie looked into Ava's dark eyes, and, though taken aback by the question, tried to add some swagger to her voice. "I have some moves."

Ava quirked up her eyebrows. "I'd like to see those some time." She shot Charlie a quick wink and redirected her attention to the dancers while swaying her hips with a bit more abandon—seemingly not caring that she frequently brushed against Charlie's side while doing so. Charlie, on the other hand, cared a great deal.

The dancers performed two numbers to grand applause from the crowd, after which Abe took the floor and made a speech. Charlie tried to listen, but all she could focus on was the way she felt with Ava standing so close to her.

"I'm going to find Michelle. I need to ask her something," Liz said when the crowd broke apart after Eisenberg's speech. Liz stared at Charlie a fraction longer than was necessary when making a simple announcement like that, then turned on her heels and left Charlie alone with Ava.

"Now would be the perfect time to bust some moves," Ava said. The music had come back on, playing a sixties soul song that Charlie couldn't remember the title of.

Charlie looked around for Sandra, but she was deep

in conversation with a woman Charlie recognized from meetings with EBC.

"Come on, Charlie. Show me what you've got." Ava grabbed her by the wrist and dragged her onto the corner of the patio that doubled as a dance floor. A few brave people were already gyrating their hips and throwing their hands in the air. Ava let go of Charlie's hand and joined them, flipping her long hair from left to right as she found the beat.

Charlie had no choice. She had to dance with Ava. It was hardly a chore. Charlie started moving to the rhythm of the music and inched closer and closer to Ava. Perhaps this song would be followed by a slow one and—

"I love this song," Ava said. Her dress whipped up and down as she danced, revealing some knee and, once in a while, a little bit of thigh. They danced alongside each other wordlessly for another song. When Charlie spotted a waiter with a full tray of glasses she grabbed two and offered one to Ava.

"The most fun I've had on an ordinary Thursday night in a long time," Charlie said.

"You *do* have moves, Charlie," Ava said.

"Not too bad yourself." Only last night, Charlie had watched a re-run of *Knives Out*, comparing how Ava licked her spoon on TV to how she did it in real life.

"Do you want to sit down for a bit?" Ava asked.

"Sure." Instead of heading to the cluster of tables skirting the patio, Ava led her in the direction of the swimming pool where two sun loungers sat side by side.

Ava draped herself onto one in an elegant fashion Charlie could only aspire to. Charlie sat and twirled her glass between her fingers.

"I started reading *Crying Rivers* again," Ava said. "It's a different experience to read a book when you've met the author."

"I watched a re-run of *Knives Out* last night," Charlie said. "I agree. Also a totally different experience."

Ava laughed. "It's hardly the same." Her head rested on her palm and she looked so relaxed.

Charlie drank from her champagne to calm her nerves. Compared to this, dancing with Ava had been easy. "My extensive research has shown that you lick a spoon with more abandon off camera," Charlie said, trying very hard to keep her gaze on Ava. She looked away nonetheless.

"I do everything with more abandon off camera. But…" Ava paused to sip from her drink. "When we start shooting the next season, I'll try to throw in a really good spoon lick for you, Charlie." Ava laughed, and the sound was so pleasing to the ear, Charlie wanted to make her laugh again. Pronto.

"You can be sure I'll be watching."

"I wanted to ask you a more serious question, actually," Ava said, but kept the smile on her face.

Charlie slanted her head in anticipation.

"You're with Lynch & Archer, aren't you? They've offered me a very generous contract to write a book."

"Really? That's great news."

"I don't know if I want to do it. Every other person who has been on TV for more than five minutes has a book out these days. At the risk of sounding snobbish… I like literature. Not flimsy celebrity memoirs." Ava pushed herself up from the lounger. Perhaps the direction this conversation was taking warranted a less frivolous pose.

"I, on the other hand, do love a juicy memoir," Charlie said.

"You're not the only one. Those books sell like hot cakes, which makes the proposal very tempting, but… I don't know. I guess I want to offer something more. Something with a bit more depth."

"If you're writing the book, you can give it as much depth as you like," Charlie said.

"But nobody wants to read that. All everybody wants is for me to dish on my past relationships and to find out about how I made it in Hollywood." Ava scrunched her lips together.

Charlie would love to read Ava's memoir. "You'll have to add some never-before-revealed secrets as well, of course, to help the marketing go viral."

"Of course." Ava nodded, but the smile was back on her face. "Well, this is a first world problem."

"This whole town is a first world problem," Charlie said.

"There you are." Sandra appeared next to them. "You don't want to miss Abe cutting into a gigantic cake in the shape of a TV."

"A 60-inch flat screen, I hope?" Charlie asked.

"That man loves television. That's all I can say," Sandra said earnestly.

Ava rose and put a hand on Charlie's shoulder. "Let's continue this conversation later."

They all walked back to where the party was happening. Sandra hadn't lied. A huge TV-shaped cake with EBC's logo on the screen stood in the middle of the living room.

Charlie found Liz again and, for the remainder of the night, every time she looked for Ava, she was talking to someone else. Charlie didn't want to be that person who cut into a conversation between strangers. They would need to find another time to continue their own chat. Charlie couldn't wait.

CHAPTER FIVE

Charlie was sitting in Nick and Jason's back yard, when Nick asked, "What do you mean you just ran into Ava at a party? Which party and when?" Nick tapped his fingers on the tabletop nervously.

Charlie loved how captive an audience he was—especially when it came to matters like these. She told him about the EBC party at Abe Eisenberg's house, then added, "We had a lovely chat." Charlie had replayed the part of the evening she'd spent with Ava over and over in her head a million times since then. "And I might be very, very wrong about this, but... I couldn't shake the impression she was flirting with me a little."

Nick's eyes widened. "Well, you might be right, Charlie. Because look at this." Nick tapped on his phone screen a few times, then presented it to Charlie.

Could you pass me Charlie Cross's number, please, Nickie?

"Oh... My... God!" Charlie gave her best desperate housewife impression. "When did she send this?"

"Just before you arrived. Jason is my witness. I would never keep such an important development from you for longer than thirty seconds, but since you were coming over, I thought it could wait until you were here." He swirled the red wine in his glass.

"Have you texted anything back?"

"No. I wanted to ask you first. This is Hollywood,

darling. Private telephone numbers are a precious commodity."

Charlie thought she might hyperventilate. "Send it to her now, for Christ's sake."

"Why is this so thrilling?" Jason asked. "I'm getting all excited as well, Charlie."

Charlie had to stop herself from going into directions too implausible to fathom. "She is one hundred percent straight, right?" she blurted out in response.

Nick rolled his eyes. "You and your silly percentages." He finally released his fingers from around the stem of his glass. "When are you going to let that go? You should know better. Not to mention that it's highly disrespectful to a lot of people."

"Why?" Charlie asked. "It's my own private system. I'm not judging anyone with it, only protecting myself."

"Yeah, yeah, yeah, whatever." Nick fixed her with a stern stare. "Here's the deal. No more talk of percentages tonight and I'll send Ava your number straightaway—no pun intended."

"Yes, please do." Charlie all but shouted. She didn't know what to do with herself. Apart from, perhaps, burst out of her skin with elation. Nick typed on his phone for a few seconds.

"There. Done."

Charlie couldn't keep her eyes off his phone in case it lit up with a reply.

"Try to keep cool, honey," Nick said. "Besides, Jason has news. It's not all about you, you know?"

Charlie looked at Jason. He was so tall and dark. If Nick could snag a man that handsome, why should Charlie not give in—if only for a fraction of a second—to a fantasy of her by Ava Castaneda's side? This city was made of fantasies. And she needed something to do in her spare time, in those lonely hours before falling asleep at night. It beat dredging up memories of her bygone life with Jo.

"I got back from New York this morning…" He paused strategically.

Charlie already knew where this conversation was headed, but she was in an excellent mood—her gaze still trained on Nick's phone—and suppressed the obligatory sigh that always accompanied news of Jo.

"Where I met up with Jo, as I always do."

Nick and Jason had been Jo's friends first. She had befriended Jason when they'd become colleagues ten years ago. Despite the ugliness of their breakup and Charlie's firm conviction that none of it had been her fault, Charlie could hardly hold it against Jason that he kept in touch with her ex.

"Her firm wants to send her to LA for a few months. She designed Alex Duffy's penthouse on Park Avenue, and he requested her personally to update his house in the Hills."

"Are you fucking kidding me?" Charlie's good mood was melting like snow in the LA sun. "No way is she coming here."

"It's hardly something she can refuse," Nick said. "She has an in with the big money. She'd be a fool to say no."

"What about me?"

"What about *you*?" Nick said. Jason would never say something like that to her. He might think it, but he'd never voice it out loud. "It's been nearly ten months since you broke up."

Nine months and twenty days, to be exact. She looked at Jason instead, hoping to find some sympathy.

"Jo did ask if I thought you would be comfortable with it."

"I hope you said no." Charlie was getting caught in the familiar self-pity spiral again.

"Sweetie, it's not up to you. You can't deny your ex such a huge boost to her career just because your feelings might get the teensiest bit hurt when she's in town. Grow up."

Jason put a hand on Nick's arm. "Lay off her, honey."

"No, Jase, come on. How long has this been going on?" Nick looked from Jason to Charlie. "Yes, she broke up with you. Yes, she's in a relationship with a man now. These things happen. Such is life. And don't for one more second keep on pretending that you had nothing to do with your relationship falling apart. You basically drove her into Christian's arms."

Charlie just sat there, her lips parted in an astounded crack. Had Nick actually said these things to her? Or had she entered a parallel universe, where the past week—the first week since arriving in LA when things were going her way—had not happened. Where her ex was coming to town and the person she considered her best friend had just said it was her fault Jo had gone back to men?

"Don't mind him, Charlie," Jason, always the peacemaker, said, "he's a bit on edge." He leaned in. "He didn't get the part in *Dream Makers*. It went to Patrick Girardeau instead."

"Fucking French are taking over this town," Nick mumbled. He'd had high hopes to become a part of that cast, but it didn't excuse what he said about Charlie being the main cause of her relationship with Jo failing.

"I'm so sorry, Nickie. Why didn't you say?"

"I don't want to talk about it."

"Some of us prefer to sulk in silence. He'll get over it." Jason slung an arm over Nick's shoulders. "After all, he has me."

Nick let his head drop onto Jason's shoulder. Charlie thought it best not to push him. She'd ask him later about his true feelings about the breakup.

Jason directed his attention to Charlie again. "Jo will be flying over next week to take a first look at the house. I thought you should know she'll be in town, okay?"

"Is she staying with you?" Charlie asked. She loved Nick and Jason's place, with its soulful, impeccable interior and its small, lush garden. It was a place where she could relax away from bars, and other women, and people's expectations. And her own destructive thoughts.

"The company's putting her in a hotel. Plus, if she does decide to take the job, it will only be temporary. She has her life in New York."

Her life *without* me, *with* our cats and that hideously bearded man. "Whatever." Charlie wasn't ready to be the bigger person about this yet. *Yet*, she pondered. Could she even still use that word and have some credibility left after almost ten months? It wasn't that she was totally hung-up on Jo. Time had worked its magic and healed some wounds. It was just the way it all played out that left a really foul taste in her mouth.

"Charlie, I'm sorry," Nick said. "I shouldn't have said those things."

"Never mind." Charlie's gaze drifted from Nick's distraught face to his phone, which, just then, lit up.

"Oh my God," Charlie shrieked. "Is it from her?"

Nick reached for his phone and read the message. "Sorry, dear. It's from my agent. More words of consolation."

Charlie started to wonder what kind of friend she was if Nick didn't feel comfortable sharing bad news with her.

"So?" Jason said while Nick messaged his agent back, his eyebrows arched in an inquisitive bow. "I hear you joined a softball team? Any people of interest?"

Charlie had briefly stopped by "her" team's league game on Sunday morning, but her mind had been filled to the brim with thoughts and images of Ava, so she hadn't lingered. Although, during a break, Liz had assured her that after practice next Wednesday, she could join the game against the Mound Mermaids.

"I don't know yet." Charlie shrugged. "Could be." The thought of Jo spending time in LA would perhaps force her to be a bit more open-minded about dating. Josie was cute.

The buzzing of her phone startled her. She quickly fished it out of her pocket.

A message from an unknown number appeared on the screen. Charlie didn't give her phone number out freely, so it could only be one person. Her heart raced as she slid her thumb across the screen to unlock the phone.

How about that cooking lesson? (Meaning you can watch while I cook for you.) ;-) Ava C.

Too excited to speak, Charlie showed her phone to Nick and Jason. Neither one of them commented for several long seconds. Her fingers trembled so hard she nearly dropped her phone when she took it back and stared at the message a bit longer.

"How long should I wait to reply?"

"There's really no use in pretending you're going to play this cool," Nick said. "Say 'Yes, whenever you're free' already."

"I have social obligations," Charlie said jokingly.

"Yes, she has softball now." Jason nodded sagely.

They all laughed. It seemed like Nick and Jason were as nervous as Charlie.

"This is crazy." Charlie still couldn't believe she had a message from Ava Castaneda on her phone.

"By the way, Miss Cross, you never mentioned anything about a cooking lesson," Nick scolded her. "Don't you know by now that you must keep me informed about these things?"

"We engaged in some banter when I helped her with dessert. I admitted to never using my kitchen. She offered to teach me the basics."

Nick brought his hands to his face dramatically, his mouth agape between his splayed fingers. "That's it," he said, after flipping his hands away again. "All it took was a few hours in your presence, and you've erased at least one percent of her heterosexuality."

Jason slapped his husband on the back of the head playfully. "Give her a break. This is a huge moment for Charlie."

Charlie ignored Nick's last comment and started typing a reply. She erased the first three attempts.

"You're a writer. Say something cool and full of double entendres." Nick couldn't leave it alone.

"Writing has nothing to do with composing the perfect dinner-for-two acceptance text," Charlie replied. "This is much harder."

"And you'll even get to watch her in action." Nick mimicked licking a spoon. "Oh my."

I would love that. I'm free this weekend.

Charlie thought it best to keep things simple and pressed *send*.

* * *

On the way home, Charlie had to resist the urge to pinch herself several times to make sure she wasn't dreaming. She had a date with Ava Castaneda on Friday evening. She would be in Ava's house, watching Ava cook, and then eating with Ava while overlooking the ocean.

It was only Tuesday. What was she going to do with herself until then?

Charlie had barely made it through the door of her

house, when her phone buzzed again. Another message from Ava.

I'm still reading Crying Rivers. It's still different from the first time I read it.

A huge grin spread across Charlie's face. She plopped down in the sofa and tried to come up with a suitable response.

How many spoons will you lick for me on Friday?

Charlie wasn't entirely sure Ava had been flirting with her at the party last Thursday—it could just be her personality—but Charlie was certain that *she* was entering the realm of flirty texting. It was so much easier to keep her cool over the phone. Besides, Ava was straight. And sometimes, befriending someone required a little platonic flirting.

It took a while for Ava to respond. To keep herself from concluding that she'd been too forward with her last message, Charlie checked Ava's Instagram account to see if anything new had appeared since the last time she'd visited. Ava had posted an arty picture of her dinner—roast chicken had never looked so scrumptious.

Just as Charlie pressed the heart-shaped button icon to like Ava's picture, her phone rang. The sudden chime startled Charlie so much, she dropped the phone in her lap. When she picked it up, *Ava Castaneda* lit up the screen in big, bright letters.

"Hello," Charlie said, trying to sound much more confident than she felt.

"I can lick as many as you want, Charlie," Ava said, "but that's the second time you've abruptly changed the subject as soon as I mentioned *Crying Rivers*. Would you like to talk about it?"

"I guess talking to you is too distracting," Charlie said.

"Oh yeah? Why's that? And you're forbidden to mention the word spoon."

Was this flirting? Was this something else? "You're right," Charlie confessed. "I don't enjoy talking about it very much. But, speaking of books… your potential one to be more precise. Why don't you use the cooking angle? Your Instagram is full of the most mouthwatering pictures of food. You can tell your life story through food anecdotes. I assume you have plenty of those." Charlie was just improvising, and trying not to come across too flirty.

"I've actually thought about doing something food-related, but not quite like this. Thank you, Charlie."

"You're welcome." Charlie relaxed a little.

"I look forward to having you over on Friday," Ava said. "And I'll try not to mention your book." She chuckled into the telephone.

After this call, Charlie would surely need a counseling session with both Liz and Nick. "And I won't so much as glance at a spoon."

"We'll see about that," Ava said. "Goodnight, Charlie."

"Goodnight." They hung up and Charlie sat staring at her phone for a good long while. She wasn't that dense. This *was* flirting. Ava was flirting with her and in a few days Charlie would have dinner at her gorgeous house in Malibu. Charlie was simultaneously elated and scared to death.

She went on Instagram again and checked her own account—if she checked Ava's one more time she surely wouldn't get any sleep tonight. She scrolled through her notifications and, to her surprise, Ava had commented on one of Charlie's pictures. It was a snapshot of the paperback version of the latest *Underground* book. *Crying*

Rivers is still my favorite.

CHAPTER SIX

"Is it a date?" Liz asked with a very serious expression on her face.

"No, of course not." Charlie had managed to drag her co-worker and new teammate away from the others. Softball practice had ended, and she might have exploded if she didn't tell another human being about her plans. She and Nick had been texting feverishly since the night before, but Nick was Nick, and he always peppered his advice with snarky comments that didn't help to still Charlie's nerves.

"Then what is it called when a woman you've just met offers to cook you dinner at her home?" Liz looked puzzled. "A woman who I witnessed flirting with you with my very own eyes, I might add," Liz said.

"Erm, friendship," Charlie offered. "She knows I'm relatively new to town, so..." Charlie didn't believe what she was saying any more than Liz, but her head would explode if she let herself get carried away on the idea of dating Ava.

"I can ask around for you, you know?" Liz huddled a little closer. "Ruffle some branches of the lesbian gossip tree and see what falls to the ground."

Charlie arched her eyebrows. "The what?"

"I was born and bred here, Charlie. I know... things. I know who to talk to about more secretive subject matters."

Charlie chuckled. "That's all right." Although, if she

was completely honest with herself, the thought had crossed her mind. Percentages aside, Charlie knew all too well about sexual fluidity and the gray scale, and, even more importantly, about the pressure to keep up appearances.

"Your call." Liz's earnest demeanor couldn't be shaken. She obviously meant business. For some reason, this was a big deal to her.

"Do you have any examples of celebrities who are perceived as heterosexual but aren't, according to your... tree?" Charlie had to ask.

"Do you have a spare hour or two so I can list them all?" Liz's tone didn't show any trace of lightening up any time soon.

"Despite having a busy job, I do have some spare time."

"I was just joking," Liz said, although her face indicated she was doing anything but. "I can't give you that information. I can only do so if I deem it morally responsible. In Ava's case, it would be."

"Fine," Charlie acquiesced with a flutter in her stomach. "Shake the tree for me."

"You got it, buddy." Liz ended with a wink, as though they now shared a huge secret. "So, what about Josie?"

Charlie scanned the women who were gathered around a table a few feet away from them, bottles of water and beer scattered between them. "Last I heard, she was in on a bet with her friends Andrea and Tiff about who could seduce me first."

"Really?" Liz appeared genuinely shocked. "I'll sort them out."

They returned to join the others but, all through the banter, jokes, and the occasional crossing of her glance with Josie's, Charlie could only think of one thing.

* * *

By the time Charlie left work on Friday evening, Liz had not been able to confirm any suspicions about Ava. According to Liz, this meant that she was either extremely careful or she was simply plain old straight.

This information didn't ease Charlie's nerves as she drove to Malibu after two showers and a frustrating hour of sighing in front of the mirror because she really didn't have anything to wear to a casual dinner party with a woman who she wished was gay but, in her heart, knew full well was not.

She parked her car, shot herself one last glance in the rearview mirror, and headed toward Ava's house. Unlike last time, the doors didn't open as she walked up. Charlie shuffled her weight around a bit. Before she could knock, the door swung open and Ava appeared. Her long hair hung loose and was slightly windswept by the breeze.

Charlie opened her mouth to speak, but found that, at the first try, no sound came out. Mesmerized by the sight of Ava, she was unable to form coherent words.

"Welcome." Ava clearly wasn't stunned into speechlessness by Charlie's appearance as Charlie was by hers. Ava opened her arms wide—a gesture Charlie had hoped she would repeat—and Charlie stepped into her embrace.

The scent of flowers and oranges clung to Ava, and Charlie could have easily spent the rest of the evening with her arms wrapped around Ava's shapely body.

The hug didn't last nearly long enough to meet the fantasy Charlie had been entertaining since she'd received the invitation. A crash of bodies. A sudden realization. A hug fluidly transforming into a peck on the cheek and then, because it was just so plainly inevitable, a proper kiss on the lips, followed by a mad rush into Ava's bedroom and frantically tearing each other's clothes off.

Instead, she followed Ava to the kitchen, her heart in her throat, her cheeks flushed by the brief skin-on-skin contact, and her mind in shambles, because, what was really going on? Yes, Charlie was here to enjoy Ava's company and food, but her main mission for the evening was to find out exactly why Ava had invited her. Was she really only here to talk about books and to pick up some cooking tips?

"I've decided to make something semi simple, so it's easy for you to participate." Ava leaned against the kitchen counter. "I could have opted for really simple, but something tells me you can handle it, Charlie."

The way Ava pronounced her name—which objectively speaking, probably wasn't that different from the way Nick or Liz pronounced it—quickened her pulse as though it were a slow caress along her body. The sort of promise that set her blood on fire.

She should have "taken the pressure off" before coming to Ava's house. She'd tried, but something had kept her from finishing. The ball of nerves coiled in her stomach, perhaps. Charlie couldn't exactly pinpoint what had stopped her. The mere thought of coming here, on this "non-date date" with Ava, had her limbs paralyzed and her fingers had gone on strike.

So, now, here she stood, blazing with held-back desire, while Ava shot her an encouraging smile.

"But first," Ava said, "we drink. What did you bring?"

Charlie handed her the bottle of 1999 Chateau Margaux. Because of her job, Ava was very vocal in interviews about her food and wine preferences. It hadn't been hard for Charlie to figure out what her favorite wine was.

"Damn." Ava looked at Charlie from under her lashes.

The main lyric of the song "Bedroom Eyes" flashed through Charlie's mind.

Ava set the bottle on the counter and offered Charlie the corkscrew. "Will you do the honors? This probably needs to breathe for a while."

Opening wine was Charlie's most-practiced activity in any kitchen, so being asked to do so now boosted her confidence somewhat. For some reason, she always found comfort in removing the cork from an excellent bottle of wine.

Their fingers touched briefly, and another jolt of pure desire—there really was no point in denying what it was—entered Charlie's bloodstream. As she drove the screw into the cork, she told herself not to drink too much. She would hate to make a fool of herself. This was a "friendship date," after all. Friends didn't lust after each other the way she was lusting after Ava in that very moment. She decided that the time it took to open the bottle was the exact amount of time she was allowed to get a grip on herself.

She wasn't an impressionable teenager anymore. She was a thirty-eight-year-old woman in the prime of her life and the height of her writing career. She hadn't landed in Hollywood as a fluke. She'd come up with the idea of one of the most-hyped TV shows of the decade. A show for which Elisa Fox was making the leap from movies to television—she wasn't the first movie star to do so, but she was certainly the biggest.

"Let's sit outside for a bit first," Ava said. "We'll have the wine with dinner. I have this." She held up a bottle of Cristal.

Oh, Jesus. Small sips only! "Excellent." She grinned broadly.

Just like last time, the view of the ocean took her breath away. Ava poured her a glass of champagne, and they stood staring into the distance for a few minutes.

"It's stunning," Charlie said. "You're so lucky to live here."

"I know. Though it's a step down from Abe Eisenberg's mansion," Ava said.

"He doesn't have the beach view, though. And you should see my backyard," Charlie said.

"Maybe one day…" Ava mused. By her tone of voice, Ava didn't need an answer. "Are you renting?" Ava inquired.

"Yep. I have a place in West Hollywood."

"Of course you do."

Charlie had no idea what that was supposed to mean. Either way, real estate was not a topic she was very passionate about. If and when she decided to choose LA as her permanent place of residence, she might buy a house. Regardless, she didn't have the funds for a place by the ocean. Not to mention, thinking of houses in Hollywood made her mind wander to Jo's imminent arrival.

"Let's sit," Ava moved toward the seating area.

They shared a two-seater lounge chair that faced the ocean, a comfortable gap between their bodies.

"I thought we'd make a simple pasta sauce." Ava turned her face toward Charlie. "I mean, unless you want me to, I don't really want to teach you how to cook. I just used that as an excuse to invite you here."

Loud fireworks in Charlie's brain prevented her from coming up with a decent reply. Instead, she cocked her head to the side and studied Ava for further signs of flirting. The slightly crooked smile was there, as well as a little mischief sparkling in her eyes. Charlie might have been severely out of practice, but she did know what flirting looked and sounded like, especially when it stared her in the face like this.

"I'm sorry." Ava filled the silence. "Did I make you uncomfortable?"

"No, no, of course not." Charlie stammered. "Just took me by surprise, that's all."

Ava gave her a warm chuckle. "I'm quite a direct person. Not all the way, but 'quite.'" She locked her gaze on Charlie, who concluded that Liz's research must have been inadequate.

"I'm not all that interested in learning how to cook tonight," Charlie said. "For all I care, we can order pizza."

"Hmm." Ava took a quick drink. "I'm not sure if I should be offended or flattered by that."

"Really?" Charlie's flirting ability started to come back. "I think you know how much I enjoyed your cooking."

"Fair enough. In that case, I'm flattered that you prefer my company over my food."

"FYI, I have an excellent pizza delivery place on speed dial." She followed up by sinking her teeth into her bottom lip. If Ava was flirting, there was no way Charlie wasn't going to give as good as she got.

"No need. I have a freezer full of goodies." Ava drank the rest of her champagne and set the glass on the table in front of her, looking away from Charlie and thus breaking a bit of the tension building between them.

"Can I ask you something... personal?" Charlie couldn't wait much longer to get some answers.

"Of course." Ava reached for the bottle and topped up Charlie's glass, then refilled her own.

"I'm certainly not gullible enough to believe anything a gossip magazine publishes, but... were you and Eric ever, erm, together?"

Ava gave her a careful smile. "I do wonder why you would ask me that."

Charlie huffed out a nervous chuckle. "I don't mean to pry—" she started to say, until Ava held up her hand.

"It's okay." Her smile broadened a bit. "I know why

you're asking." She let one arm fall into her lap, which made her loose summer dress shift to the right a bit, putting her knee on display.

If it was a distraction maneuver, it worked.

"The answer is yes. Eric and I fell in love not long after he joined *Knives Out* ten years ago. We had a turbulent affair that lasted five years. It wasn't nearly as dramatic as *US Weekly* would like you to believe. Because of work, we had to remain friendly after it ended. Which wasn't easy at first, but now we're excellent pals. I consider him one of my best friends."

Charlie schooled her features into a quizzical expression. "That must have been hard though, having to work with him after breaking up?" She considered her own situation. She couldn't even be in the same city as Jo—although soon she would have to be.

"During the course of our relationship, we broke up so many times. It was actually a relief when we finally decided to put a stop to it. We've both moved on since then. We've seen other people, and we've firmly progressed into the 'friends only' space." Ava looked out over the ocean for a few seconds, as though reminiscing about her time with Eric. "We are both very direct and very passionate people. It was simply too much drama all the time when we were together. The fights we had... They were epic." Ava grinned as if the conversation had stirred some pleasant memories in her. "But we can laugh at all that now." She returned her gaze to Charlie and asked, "How about you? The WeHo lesbians must be going crazy for you?"

Charlie chuckled. "WeHo lesbians?"

"Nick tells me things."

"Oh really?" Charlie made a mental note to give him hell tomorrow if she found out he'd been talking about her behind her back.

"Not about you specifically. He tells me things in

general. You know how he likes to instruct people on gay culture and all that."

"I don't need instructing anymore." Charlie was about to finish her second glass of champagne and detected a pang of hunger in her stomach. "But I guess you might." The champagne made her a little bolder than she would have been sober.

"Touché." Ava tilted her glass toward Charlie's.

Charlie obliged and clinked the rims of their glasses together. "How about that pizza?" she asked. She needed some food if she was going to play this remotely cool at all.

Ava nodded.

There were plenty of videos on YouTube of Ava cooking. Charlie had probably seen them all. "I've seen you dice onions with humanly impossible speed on TV, and I'm already properly impressed." Charlie couldn't shake the impression that Nick might have said something to Ava after he'd sent her Charlie's number.

"Then let me see what I can find." Ava rose.

"Anything you serve will be a feast for me." Charlie straightened her posture. "Can I help?"

"You can finish that bottle of Cristal and bring the wine out." Ava's dress was low cut and dipped seductively between her breasts.

"I'm on it," Charlie said, although she wouldn't touch anymore of that champagne.

CHAPTER SEVEN

Ava had heated up a scrumptious pasta sauce from her well-stocked freezer, and they sat eating spaghetti side-by-side as the sun set in front of them. On Knives Out, Ava was well known—and much liked—for how expressively she enjoyed food, throwing in a very vocal 'mmm' and 'aaaah' as she tasted the dishes the contestants prepared.

Ava seemed to be thoroughly enjoying her own food now as well, judging from the sounds coming from her side of the table.

The wine, although much posher than the dish they were eating, complemented the food beautifully, and Charlie's champagne buzz receded. By the time the sun was a mere orange glow on the horizon, she had regained a firm grip on her behavior.

"Has Nick told you anything about me?" Charlie asked, figuring it was a fair question.

"He told me you were single," Ava said. "And that you went through a bit of a nasty breakup prior to moving to Los Angeles."

"All true." Charlie decided to follow Nick's advice from the week before and avoid the subject of her ex. She swallowed and said, "But that's all water under the bridge now."

"But you are still single?" Ava asked.

"Very." Charlie took on a more relaxed pose, holding the belly of her wine glass between her fingers. "You?"

"Yep."

"I've joined a lesbian softball team, though." Charlie wanted to kick herself for saying that. Way to play it cool. It didn't even make any sense in the context of the conversation.

"Is that a euphemism for something?" Ava asked. "If it is, I didn't get the reference." She didn't chuckle as such, but Charlie could easily make out the amusement in her voice.

"There's a girl on the team…" Charlie continued, because she needed to give some sort of explanation for what she'd just blurted out. When she took a second to actually *think* about what she'd said, however, it was the last thing she wanted to talk about.

"Do spill." Ava pushed her chair back a bit and turned so she had a good view of Charlie's face.

Since she was already in the conversation, it was as good a way as any to learn more about Ava's intentions. "We haven't really talked that much. I only just joined the team." Charlie didn't have anything meaningful to add without making something up. She certainly didn't want to tell Ava about the Terrible Three and their bet. "It's nothing really. My mind's been too preoccupied with other matters, I guess."

"The show?" Ava sat there all innocent, her face aglow in the light of a candle, her eyes dark and shiny.

"I guess that's almost out of my hands now." As passionate as Charlie was about her work, and in particular the TV show she had relocated to Hollywood for, she didn't want to talk about it. She decided it was time to ask the only question she really wanted answered. "We've been dancing around this all night." She found Ava's eyes. "Why did you invite me here tonight? Just me, on what feels a whole lot like a date."

"Ah." Ava gave a slow nod as she sucked in her cheek. "I thought you'd never ask."

Nerves flared in Charlie's gut, and she poured them some more wine to help her regain focus.

"I enjoy spending time with you. It's really as simple as that," Ava brought her newly refilled glass to her lips.

As simple as that? "So... you want to befriend me?"

"Yes." Ava nodded again. "For starters." She looked at Charlie over the rim of her glass.

"But... I... I guess, I don't understand." Charlie took a few big gulps to calm herself down.

"I like you, Charlie Cross. Is that really so hard to comprehend?"

"Well, no, but, you see..." Charlie took a deep breath. She was sick of all this stammering. "I like you, too, but probably in a very different way than you, erm, like me."

"I agree that the word 'like' can have various definitions in this context, but I'm also fairly certain that the way I like you isn't that dissimilar to how you like me."

Charlie broke out into the biggest smile.

"Come on." Ava put her glass on the table. "Take off your shoes."

"For real?" There was direct, and then there was extremely forward. Not that Ava had asked her to get naked, but they had to start somewhere.

"Let's go onto the beach." Ava rose and took off her shoes.

"Oh. Sure." Charlie fumbled with her laces longer than she normally would, and by the time she got up, Ava had already walked down the wooden path leading to the ocean. She waited for Charlie where the path gave way to sand.

"No point in living here if all you're going to do is watch the waves." She held out her hand and Charlie took it. It was by far the most romantic moment of her life.

Hand-in-hand, they walked to the shore line. Darkness had almost completely settled, but there was a half-moon ahead and a smattering of stars. She could never see stars like that in WeHo.

The sand was cool between her toes, Ava's hand was hot in hers, and Charlie employed all her mental strength to keep her warped mind from ruining this moment. She was on a stretch of deserted beach with Ava Castaneda, the water lapping at their feet, the moon casting an idyllic glow around them.

"What do you think, Charlie?"

"About what?"

They stopped walking, and the wind blew through Ava's hair as she faced Charlie and reached for her other hand.

"Is this the perfect setting for our first kiss or can we do better?"

"We most certainly can not." The words came out as an urgent whisper. Charlie was not a short woman, but with her endless model legs, Ava stood much taller than her.

Ava took a step toward her and a hint of her perfume wafted into Charlie's nose. They brought their hands up, fingers intertwined. All Charlie saw was Ava's face, her head slanting toward her, her full lips curved into a hint of smile.

When their lips met, Charlie felt as though she were floating above the sand. As though all her dreams were coming true in the instant their mouths found each other. The kiss was close-lipped for the first few seconds, until their mouths opened in unison, and Ava's tongue slipped inside. Charlie didn't pay attention to the warning signs flashing in her mind, and gave herself up entirely to the sensation of kissing Ava on a moonlit beach in Malibu.

Ava released her hold on Charlie's fingers, dropping them to her side for a moment until Charlie put them on

Ava's waist and tugged her closer. With her tongue still invading Ava's mouth, their lips, ever so slowly, parted for a break, and Ava made the same approving noises as when she ate a delicious dish.

Ava curved her arms around Charlie's neck and pulled her even tighter against her. Their bodies met in a soft embrace, and their lips followed.

Charlie's knees gave way a little the second time Ava's tongue slipped its way inside her mouth. She folded her arms around Ava's back and pressed the length of her body against her. Charlie's pulse quickened at the extended body contact—Ava's breasts pushed into hers, just above her nipples. The sea roared, and soon, Charlie grew as wet as the waves at her feet. But, her mind refused to stay out of it and simply enjoy this moment as pure pleasure—as the realization of a fantasy. What was Ava experiencing? Was her blood throbbing in her veins? Did she want to rip off Charlie's clothes as much as Charlie wanted to let that dress slide off Ava?

It seemed highly unlikely.

Still, when they broke from their second lip-lock, a huge grin spread on Charlie's lips. When she glanced at Ava, the same kind of smile reflected back at her.

"Do you want to go inside?" Ava asked.

"Sure," Charlie said, although she was convinced it would break the spell. Because, perhaps, wrapped in darkness on this beach, surrounded by sand and ocean, they could have been equals for the few minutes their lips met, but once inside Ava's house, everything would change. Charlie's mind was already doing the changing.

Ava grabbed her hand again, and this time the contact shot through Charlie a million times stronger than before. Her body wanted to pull Ava to her, to press kiss after kiss onto her mouth, her nose, those cheekbones, and then lower. But Charlie's mind would never allow that. Ava might have kissed her, but that didn't make her a lesbian.

Ava dragged her toward the house. They quickly wiped their feet on a coarse door mat, before they tumbled into the kitchen, their bodies meeting again, as well as their lips.

Without a doubt, this date had exceeded all Charlie's expectations. Ava had given her a loud and clear response to the question she had come here with. She wanted to take Charlie to bed. It couldn't happen. Not without first acquiring a whole lot more knowledge about Ava's motivations and past.

Ava traced her lips from Charlie's mouth to her ear and whispered, "Do you want to stay?"

"God, I do." Charlie moaned. Every cell in her body was saturated with desire. "But I can't."

"Why not?" Ava's voice was a breathy groan in her ear.

"Because…" Charlie put some distance between them. "I barely know you." Liz's words flitted through her mind. *Either Ava is very careful or just plain old straight.* "And you're not… into women."

"When I do this," Ava stepped closer again, bringing her hands to the back of Charlie's head and letting her fingers roam through her hair, "does it really make you feel like I'm not into women?" Ava slid the tip of her tongue over the shell of Charlie's ear. Heat crashed through Charlie. But her mind had always been much stronger than any desire.

"We have to stop now," she said, her voice a bit louder than she wanted.

Ava pulled back with a brusque movement and didn't say anything for a second, just regarded Charlie with those dark eyes. "I'm sorry. I got a bit carried away there." She flashed Charlie a seductive smile. "We haven't even had dessert yet."

"I think I'd better go." Charlie squared her

shoulders. Her mind was winning more and more ground in the battle with her heart.

"Now? Oh, Charlie." Ava cocked her head and raised her hand to just above her chest. "Look, I'm sorry. I came on too strong. It's how I am sometimes. I wanted to kiss you, and I went for it without taking your feelings into consideration. You're right. We barely know each other. But we can't change that if you go." She dropped her hand to her side. Sometime during their embrace, her dress had gotten wrinkled. "Stay." It sounded more like a plea than anything else. "Let's talk."

"I'm sorry, Ava. I can't. I—" What could Charlie possibly say next without sounding like the biggest fool? I've barely recovered from my previous relationship, and I have no idea how to cope with something as powerful as *this* going wrong? And, really, how could it not?

"Fine." Something in Ava's face changed. She probably wasn't accustomed to rejection. "But you shouldn't drive. You drank too much. I'll call you a taxi."

Charlie couldn't argue with that. "Thanks," she muttered. She wanted to apologize again, but Ava left the kitchen to find her phone.

Charlie retrieved her shoes. As she laced them up, her chest tightened. Was she really saying no to Ava Castaneda?

"Taxi will be here in ten minutes." Ava appeared in the doorframe. "You might as well finish the wine."

Charlie rose and walked over to Ava, but kept a safe distance. "Please believe me, this has nothing to do with you, Ava. This is all me. There are just certain… things… I—" Charlie got stuck. Her brain failed to produce any more valid words.

"It's okay. You don't have to explain."

"I find you extremely attractive." Charlie felt like a complete fool. She didn't belong here, in this city where straight women hit on her. "I just…" But Charlie couldn't explain the blockage in her heart, and the way her mind operated.

Ava poured them both some wine and pushed a glass in Charlie's direction.

Charlie stared at it, unable to move. Had Jo really done such a number on her that it made her incapable of accepting Ava's advances?

"I've had enough. I'll go wait outside." Apart from being paralyzed by the fear of having her heart broken all over again, Charlie was also mortified by how she'd allowed this evening to play out.

"There's no need for that, Charlie." The wattage of Ava's smile had dimmed considerably.

"Thanks for dinner." Charlie really needed to get away from Ava's gaze.

"Pleasure," Ava said and narrowed her eyes.

"I really need to go now," Charlie took a step backward, then turned around and walked the short route through the house to the front door. After she let it fall shut behind her, she took a deep breath, adamant not to fall apart on Ava's doorstep. She double-checked if her car was locked properly, and waited, the half-moon overhead nothing but a reminder of what had happened on the beach.

CHAPTER EIGHT

"Please come with me," Charlie pleaded.

"You can use my car service, but I really can't, darling," Nick said. "Jason and I are being interviewed by *Vanity Fair.*"

Charlie remembered now. He needed to prepare, so she probably shouldn't take up too much of his time. "I… can't go back there on my own."

"Of course, you can," Nick said, impatient. Hangers slid along racks in the background. "It will give you a chance to talk."

"She hasn't called you?" Charlie asked again.

"Nope." Nick sighed. "Look, sweetie, don't make too big a deal out of this, okay? I know how you are and how you can get lost in your head. From what you've told me, Ava likes you. Just be adult about it." There was some fumbling on the other end of the line, and Charlie thought the connection had been lost until Nick said, "I really have to go. I'll send a car over. Go now, before you blow things up more in your head."

"Thanks, Nickie. Charm the pants off the VF lady."

"You know me, dear," he said and hung up.

Ten minutes later, a black town car pulled up outside of Charlie's house. An hour later, they arrived at Ava's. Charlie asked the driver not to tell Ava she was in the car with him. With a bit of luck, Ava would assume Charlie had sent someone to pick up her car, and she would stay inside her house.

By the time they reached the end of the driveway, her heart pounded relentlessly in her throat. To Charlie's relief, the front door was closed and all was quiet around her red Mini Cooper. She'd bought it on a whim after first arriving. In New York, Charlie didn't have a car, but living in LA required a person to have one if she didn't want to spend half her life waiting for a taxi.

"Thanks," Charlie said as she climbed out of the car. "No need to wait." She had to wait for the town car to turn around and drive away before she could leave. She'd only just unlocked her car when a voice sounded behind her.

"Were you really going to sneak off?"

Charlie turned around. Ava wore jeans and a T-shirt and no makeup. In the Saturday morning light, she looked even more stunning than she had under the moon.

"No, no, of course not." Charlie lied.

"Do you want to come in? Have you had breakfast?"

This was exactly why Charlie asked Nick to come with her. She could hardly run off twice in fewer than twenty-four hours.

"Sure, I'll come in." She tried to sound confident.

Once seated at the breakfast bar with a steaming mug of coffee in front of her, Charlie exhaled and tried to launch into an acceptable apology. "Look, Ava, I—"

"Before you say anything, Charlie, I owe you an apology. I came on too strong and overreacted when you didn't reciprocate my advances. I was a bit crazy last night. I shouldn't have let you walk out like that. You were clearly upset."

At hearing this, Charlie was finally able to exhale fully and relax a bit more. She had practiced what she was going to say, repeating the words as if she were auditioning for a movie part—the one of uptight, zero-tolerance lesbian. She was in the right town for it.

"It was my fault entirely. I should have handled it better. I mean, you're gorgeous. You are also a gracious host, an excellent chef, and a very kind woman. I was thrilled to be invited here again. And I, erm," Charlie hesitated, "I greatly enjoyed our kiss on the beach."

"But you have it in your head that I'm straight, and it freaked you out," Ava said.

Charlie wouldn't have put it that way, but it was accurate enough. She nodded. She was gearing up to say the words she hated to say, but they needed to be said to make this right. "Jo, my ex, left me for a man, and I'm still sort of recovering from that. Getting off with a straight woman is… not something I can do right now. No matter how gorgeous she is, how big my crush is, or how amazing a kisser she is." Charlie shook her head. "I just can't."

"Why are you so convinced I'm straight?" Ava smiled.

"It doesn't really matter if you're straight or bisexual. It's clear you're not a lesbian. I can't… put my heart on the line."

"Just like that?" For some reason, Ava continued to smile. "I'm dismissed?"

"I understand your skepticism, and I'm very familiar with all the arguments against my reasoning, but I know what I need to do to protect myself from going through what I went through after Jo again. Even though it might cost me greatly." Charlie was adamant about this, but it didn't mean her curiosity hadn't been piqued. "You don't have to tell me, of course, but, erm, have you ever been in love with a woman before?"

Ava pondered this, gazing over the rim of her cup while doing so. "In love… I'm not sure." She looked at Charlie. "I had a fling with Sandra, but we never quite managed to fall in love."

"Sandra? She's a lesbian?" Charlie hadn't picked up that vibe at all, and Ava's publicist hadn't dropped the slightest of hints.

"Not openly."

Charlie expelled a sigh. "What I'm looking for in a woman is really very straightforward. Someone out and proud and secure enough in her sexuality to not leave me for a man. Personally, I think my wish list is quite fair, but someone like Nick, for instance, never fails to give me a hard time about it. He claims I'm too rigid with my requirement that a woman be completely lesbian. He thinks I'm afraid and looking for excuses."

"And already, even after only one kiss, you're convinced that, if we were to embark on... something, I would leave you for a man in the end?" Ava narrowed her eyes. She didn't say anything else.

"It's certainly a possibility." Charlie looked into the remains of her coffee. "And once it's in my head, it's there to stay." She cut her glance to Ava. "Besides, why would someone like you be interested in someone like me?"

"What do you mean 'someone like you'?" Ava put her mug down.

"You're an ex-model. You're on TV. You could have anyone you wanted, really."

"But not you." Ava made it sound like a statement, not a question. "I make my living by how I look, Charlie. I might have picked up some cooking and presenting skills along the way, but if I'm being truly honest, all the success I've had in my life is based on my appearance. You, on the other hand, have this amazing mind out of which the most beautiful sentences are born. I find that extremely attractive." She slid off the stool she was sitting on. "I would like to show you something."

Charlie followed Ava through the living room and into an adjoining room she hadn't seen during her previous two visits. The entire space was lined with bookcases, every shelf filled to the brim.

Ava crossed the room to a case near the window. "These are arranged alphabetically. This is where I keep the Cs." She gestured with her hand to the middle shelf.

Charlie easily recognized the spines with her name printed on them. The heat of a blush crept up her neck.

"I don't just own these, Charlie. I've read every single one of them. And yes, that includes the saucy ones. I wasn't kidding when I said I was a fan." She pulled a book from the row. "I know it's not very original, but I already told you *Crying Rivers* is my favorite."

Charlie stared at the cover of her break-through novel. The one that put her on the map and made Hollywood take notice of her.

"I was going to ask you to sign it for me last night, but well, things turned out slightly differently than expected."

"Did you expect to kiss me?" Charlie gained confidence from looking at her books—and from Ava's display of fan-girl admiration.

"Not sure 'expect' is the right word, but I'd certainly thought about it." Ava thumbed through the book. It looked as if it had been read numerous times, with the corners of several pages flipped back. "This is my favorite sentence of them all." She inhaled, preparing to read out loud, but Charlie stopped her.

"Please. Don't."

"Really?" Ava glanced at her. "Okay," she quickly agreed.

"I'll sign it for you if you still want me to."

"I would really appreciate that."

Ava handed her the book. "Why don't you take it home? Sign it for me in privacy and bring it back later."

Charlie accepted it and nodded.

"I would love to get to know you better. This way,

we have to see each other again."

"You still want to be friends?"

"I promise not to throw you off guard with impromptu kisses on the beach." Ava inched closer but didn't touch. "Speaking of the beach… Do you want to stay and have a swim?"

The flush that had reached her neck earlier, headed to Charlie's cheeks. "I don't have my bathing suit with me."

"No need for that here." Ava chuckled. "I'm just kidding. I have all sizes lying around. I'm sure we can find you something."

Charlie ignored the hesitation brewing in the back of her mind. She'd made it clear to Ava that nothing could happen, but that didn't mean she couldn't at least enjoy the view of Ava in a bikini. "Okay. Why not?"

"That's the spirit." Ava came closer and gently bumped her shoulder against Charlie's. "We can always order pizza after."

A swarm of butterflies took flight in Charlie's stomach. How long would her mind be able to hold out against this onslaught of emotion and lust.

* * *

"I can set you up with Sandra, if you like," Ava said. They'd gone for a quick dip in the ocean and now lay on deck chairs overlooking its blue splendor. "Although, I must admit that might make me jealous."

Charlie felt rather self-conscious in the bathing suit Ava had lent her. It was cut out high above her thighs, and the cups of the bikini top barely kept her breasts in check. She suspected Ava had given her that one on purpose, to make her a little bit uncomfortable—and perhaps to get a good look at what lay beneath Charlie's clothes. Ava's bikini was bright red and Charlie had a lot of trouble keeping herself from staring.

"Please, don't set me up with anyone." Charlie closed her eyes.

"Then tell me about the girl you talked about last night. The one on your softball team."

"Really?" Charlie blinked her eyes open against the strong sun and regarded Ava.

"Of course. If we're going to be friends, it's only natural to talk about things like that."

The more Ava mentioned the two of them becoming friends, the less Charlie wanted to be a part of that friendship. Ava was lying half-naked beside her on a dreamy beach, and she'd told her in no uncertain terms nothing could happen in order to protect her fragile little heart. Anyone in their right mind would have a good laugh at that. But Charlie hadn't been in her right mind for a while now. Although, she had to admit, having just swum in the Pacific Ocean with Ava made the thought of Jo arriving in LA next week a little bit more bearable.

"Her name is Josie. She's a writer for a lesbian website and a comic in her spare time. I don't really know much else about her yet."

"Which website?" Ava asked, as if she would know.

"Indigo."

"I read that sometimes."

"You do?"

"Yes, Charlie." Ava suddenly sounded like a kindergarten teacher. "Is it really so hard to get it in your head that not everything is black and white? You read 'straight' media, don't you? Why wouldn't I check that website if I feel like it?"

Charlie couldn't contain herself any longer. She had to ask. "On a scale of zero to one hundred, where zero is completely straight and one hundred completely lesbian, where would you put yourself?"

"You've been dying to ask me that ever since last

night, haven't you?"

Charlie shrugged. "Maybe."

Ava smiled. She was such a good sport, really. "You first."

"Oh, that's easy. At one hundred and fifty, for sure."

Ava shook her head. "No need to overcompensate like that."

Charlie ignored her comment. "Your turn."

"So you're what they call a gold star, I take it?" Ava asked, ignoring Charlie in return.

"Yep. I pretty much knew by the time I was twelve that girls had a much bigger effect on me than boys ever could. I skipped the whole experimenting phase and had my first girlfriend when I was sixteen."

"So why the need to tack fifty extra percentage points onto your 'score'?"

"Are you mocking me?"

"Only a little." Ava's abs rippled as she laughed easily.

"I'm still waiting for your answer." Charlie was getting impatient.

"I know, but it's an impossible question to answer in a satisfactory manner. I can hardly sit here and claim to be a hundred percent, I wouldn't even consider myself to be around the fifty mark. More in the thirties, I guess. But I don't want you to freak out about that."

"Why would I freak out?"

"Because, perhaps, if I were in the upper fifties you'd consider giving me a chance... because you like me." Ava looked straight ahead, her eyes aimed at the sky, then turned on her side to lock her gaze on Charlie. "For you, I think I could be seventy-five percent though, Charlie."

"Oh for Christ's sake. Mock me all you want... This is serious for me." Then it dawned on her. The inkling she'd had the night before returned in full force. "Has Nick told you about my percentage obsession?"

Ava chuckled. "He only mentioned it briefly. He told me to ignore it if you—and these are his words, not mine—started making a fool of yourself like that."

"I can't believe this." Charlie averted her gaze. "If I'm such a joke to him, then why is he even my friend. Because he pities me, perhaps?"

"He's your friend because he adores you, Charlie. Quirks and all. And rightly so."

Although Charlie couldn't see Ava's face, she could hear a smile coming through in her voice. This morning was turning into one long flirtation going nowhere.

"I think I'm going for another swim." She pushed herself up in her chair.

"Please do. Your ass looks really good in that bikini."

Charlie looked behind her at a grinning Ava. It wasn't difficult to figure out the game she was playing. And it might very well be a game to her, but for Charlie, this was serious business.

CHAPTER NINE

Charlie missed the ball again. It swished right past her bat, straight into the catcher's mitt. To say her first league game wasn't going very well was a severe understatement.

"You're out," the umpire called, and Charlie hurried to the dugout, deflated and disappointed.

"I'm sorry for screwing up like that." She sat down next to Liz, who slapped her on the shoulder.

"Don't worry about it, buddy. This is your first game. You can hardly expect to be the star player." Liz was one of the most positive people Charlie had ever met. "That being said, you do look a little distracted, though. Hot 'friendship date'?" Liz smiled and winked at her.

"I guess that's a pretty accurate way of describing it." Charlie grinned as she leaned in and whispered, "She kissed me, though."

Liz's eyes opened even wider. "Are you kidding me?"

"Most certainly not, my friend."

"It's as though I can hear a plethora of lesbian hearts breaking this very second." Liz slapped her on the knee this time. "But good for you, buddy."

"Good? There is no way this is good for me."

Liz stared at her for a few seconds, as if computing something in her brain. "Oh, right." She nodded her understanding. "I see."

"In fact, I was thinking about asking Josie out for a

date."

"What a great idea to go for the no-strings-attached girl."

"What's that supposed to mean?"

"We'll talk later, buddy. I'm up." Liz ran onto the field, not looking back.

They lost the game, but no one seemed to mind. At the bar afterward, Charlie hung out near Josie. She had to do something to stop the never-ending reel of Ava images in her brain. Ava leaning in to kiss her. Ava tilting her head back and exposing her neck while drinking wine. Ava handing her *Crying Rivers*. Ava walking into the waves in her red bikini.

"Hey, Charlie, we need you," Sarah said. "You're single, right?" Sarah stood next to Josie.

"Rub it in, why don't you?" Charlie replied.

"There's no shame in that. In fact, this is excellent news." A few team members clapped. "The club is organizing a single's auction for charity in three weeks. If you would agree to be auctioned off, that could bring in some serious dough!"

"A single's auction?" Charlie stared at Sarah incredulously.

"You know, where people can bid to go on a date with you." A few more team members started clapping and roaring. "Tiff, Josie, and Andrea are up for grabs as well. I'd participate myself, but my lovely wife disagrees."

"No need to give an answer now, Charlie," Liz chimed in. "Sarah really is sort of springing this on you."

"No, it's fine. I'll do it."

"That's awesome!" Sarah shouted. "It's for a good cause. We're supporting a shelter for homeless teens and a lot of them are LGBT."

Charlie gazed briefly at Josie. Perhaps she should make her move now that the conversation had shifted to dating. "Then I'll be honored to put my reputation on the line." Charlie shot them all a smile.

Tiff, who stood next to her, held up her hand for a high five, and Charlie happily slapped her palm against it. She was, at last, starting to belong to some sort of community in LA.

"Can we bid on each other?" Tiff asked Sarah.

Sarah rolled her eyes at Tiff.

Just as Charlie was about to take a step in Josie's direction, Liz swooped in. "Hey, Casanova," she said while hooking her arm around Charlie's.

"Yes, boss."

"First, thanks for agreeing to do that. I was going to ask you in private so you could decline with dignity, but Sarah jumped the gun."

"Oh, it's fine. My pleasure, really."

"You say that now." Liz pulled her face into a funny pout. "We've organized these before, and it's not exactly the fairytale situation you'd like to believe it's going to be. Some of the women who bid are really loaded and willing to spend tons of cash on a date, so we keep the tradition going for charity's sake."

"Maybe I can get Nick to come over and outbid everyone to save my ass."

"Maybe, but, erm, Charlie, I wanted to talk to you about something else."

"Let me guess." Charlie sipped from her post-game beer. It had gone a bit stale and warm. "Josie?"

"I wouldn't object if you hadn't told me about Ava kissing you, but I don't want anyone's feelings getting hurt."

"Come on, Liz. She bet that she would be the first to score a date with me."

Liz held up her hands. "I know. I know. I've scolded them for that. It won't happen again."

"You're such a momma bear, Lizzie."

"Someone has to be." Liz tugged at the hem of her

shirt.

"You know I'm not interested in Ava in that way. I can't be. I'm genuinely interested in Josie."

"As long as you're not using her to... I don't know. Get your mind off someone else." Liz glanced at Charlie's beer. "Shall I get you another?" She simply couldn't help being the nicest person on the planet.

"I promise I only have the best of intentions, Lizzie Bear." Charlie pulled Liz into a hug. "And I'll get you another."

After giving Liz her fresh drink, Charlie finally walked up to Josie. "Would you like to win a bet?" she asked. It had taken her the entire softball game to come up with that opening line.

"Good one." Josie clinked the rim of her glass against Charlie's, spilling a bit of beer in the process. "Oops, sorry about that." She stared at the wet stain on Charlie's jersey.

"Don't worry. That's why washing machines were invented."

"How do you propose I win that bet?" Josie got back to the point.

"By going on a date with me, of course." Charlie smiled triumphantly.

"That's not going to win me anything, although it would be a nice start."

"What do you mean? I heard you and Tiff and Andrea had a bet on who would manage to go out with me first?" It sounded completely ridiculous when she said it out loud like that.

"Go out with you?" Josie shook her head, smiling. "I believe you might have been missinformed."

"Oh."

"Hey, we play softball after all. We're more prone to place bets on which base we can make it to."

Charlie pretended to chuckle at the lame joke.

"Never mind," she said and made to leave.

"Hold on," Josie said. "I'm sorry. I was just messing with you. My bad." She put her hand on Charlie's arm. "I make stupid jokes when I'm nervous, that's all."

"I guess we've all been there." Charlie turned to face her fully again.

"Do you want to see a movie together?" Josie asked. "I'm free tonight." She accompanied her question with an endearing smile.

Charlie expelled a dramatic breath and said, "I would love to."

* * *

Josie shared an apartment with a friend a few streets away from Charlie's place. Charlie picked her up and drove them to the theatre.

Since the first time Charlie had gone to the movies as a kid, she'd been mesmerized by how powerful a medium it was and what a trip sitting in a dark room with a bunch of strangers could be. Today, though, it didn't really matter which movie they watched together, as long as it was entertaining enough, and as an extra bonus, provided an easy topic of conversation after. Charlie let Josie pick the movie, and they ended up at a screening of *Nothing Without You*, the latest Jenna Blakely rom-com.

At first, it was thrilling to sit in the semi-dark next to someone she'd just met, their arms bumping when they reached for their drinks. As the movie inched closer to its predictable finale, Charlie had to drag herself out of reverie after reverie of sitting in a dimly lit theatre with Ava instead of Josie.

It didn't help that Josie broke out in a loud giggle at the silliest of jokes. And she was supposed to be a comic.

"That was so much fun," Josie said, when they left the theatre. "Did you enjoy it?"

"It's not really my preferred genre." Charlie tried to be diplomatic.

"What? You should have said."

"No, it's fine. As long as you enjoyed it." They walked slowly to Charlie's car.

"You get to pick where we go for drinks, then." Josie was dressed in the shortest of shorts. Not that Josie didn't have the legs for it, but Charlie would never choose to wear something so flimsy to watch a movie.

"Lux?" Charlie offered. It was a selfish choice, because then she would be able to walk home.

"That viper's nest," was all Josie said. "Half the team will be there, as well as a third of my exes."

"I have a cozy, quiet backyard," Charlie proposed next. "And a few bottles of excellent vino."

"Deal." Josie stared at her from under long, long lashes. Ava had long lashes too, but they didn't look so unnatural.

On the way to her house, Charlie scolded herself for letting Ava dominate her thoughts. She was on a date. Moreover, she was the one who had asked Josie out. She'd deliberately picked her and now here they were. It was only polite to make the most of it.

"What do you get for winning the bet?" Charlie asked before pulling into her driveway.

"Oh, it was just for the honor." Josie shot her an apologetic smile. "Despite it not being very honorable in the first place."

When she smiled like that, she looked quite kissable. Charlie smiled back as she opened the door and escorted Josie inside.

"If you could grab two glasses from that cabinet." She pointed above the sink. "I'll be right out with a lovely bottle of Pinot Noir, or do you prefer white?"

"Red's fine." Josie stretched and retrieved the glasses. "What a lovely place."

Charlie had never really considered her house lovely. The loft she'd shared with Jo in Brooklyn had been spectacular—mostly courtesy of Jo's interior decorating skills. This house came fully furnished, and didn't reflect Charlie's taste at all. It was only a temporary home for her. If *Underground* did well, and she decided to stay—which might also happen for different reasons, but she hadn't encountered those yet—she'd look for a more permanent place that she could make her own.

"Thanks." Charlie had found the bottle she wanted, unearthed a corkscrew from the drawer, and remembered her giddy nerves when she'd uncorked that bottle of wine at Ava's.

"Are you okay?" Josie enquired. "You seemed lost in thought there for a moment."

"I'm fine." Charlie led the way outside to her tiny garden.

"Oh my God," Josie exclaimed, not unlike Charlie had done silently when faced with Ava's view of the ocean. "I want to live here."

"Let's have a glass of wine first." Charlie poured and handed Josie a glass.

"No U-Haul jokes, I promise." Josie sniffed her glass like a connoisseur. "So, out with it, Charlie. Why did you pick me?"

"Wow. Have you been saving that up until now?"

"Correct. The worst that can happen at this point is you kicking me out of your house for asking untoward questions."

"The answer is rudely simple." Charlie tried the wine before continuing.

"Excellent comic timing," Josie said, a twinkle of amusement in her eye.

"Because you're my type." Charlie chewed her bottom lip, waiting to see how that would go down with Josie.

"Fair enough." Josie pulled her lips into a crooked, seductive grin. "You like exotic girls with long, black hair."

You have no idea, Charlie thought. "Oh, yes."

"Well, I have a thing for blue-eyed writers with shaggy blond hair."

"This really couldn't be working out better." The irony of her statement wasn't lost on Charlie.

"I could think of a few ways to improve the situation." Josie went into full-on flirt mode.

Just as Charlie tried to come up with a decent response, her phone vibrated urgently against her thigh. Normally, Charlie wouldn't bother checking during a date, but it was as if she could sense the text was from Ava. "My phone," she said. "Sorry." She scrunched her lips into an apologetic pout.

Josie shrugged and reached for her purse, most likely to check her messages as well.

Charlie's heartbeat picked up as she pulled her phone from her pocket. There it was, lit up on the screen. A message from Ava.

When can I have my book back?

Charlie's lips spread into a goofy smile.

"Good news?" Josie asked.

Josie's voice pulled Charlie out of another thought spiral centered around Ava. "Sorry. What?"

"That smile could melt whatever's left of the North Pole."

"Oh, yeah." Charlie chuckled. "Just a second, please." At the risk of coming across rude, she typed out her response.

Leave me alone, I'm on a date. ;-)

She wasn't sure she should actually send that to Ava, but she didn't have time to consider it for too long. She pressed *send* and put her phone screen-down on the table.

"All yours again."

"I'm not sure about that." Josie straightened her posture. "I wasn't born yesterday, Charlie, and you never once sent me anything near a smile like that. I don't mind if you're seeing other people, obviously, but witnessing that made me feel really bad for a minute."

"I assure you I'm not seeing anyone else. If I was, I wouldn't have asked you out."

"Then who was that?"

"Just a friend." The conversation jolted Charlie right out of her pleasant mood. She'd exchanged similar words with Jo too many times to let them pass her by.

"Okay, if you say so." Josie didn't look convinced.

Charlie had, in fact, spoken those exact words to Jo, in the most passive-aggressive manner possible, quite a few times during the last months of their relationship.

It was getting darker, and it was hard to ignore the faint light her screen shed onto the table, despite being upside-down. Charlie itched to check Ava's reply, but that would blow the evening entirely.

"Tell me honestly, Charlie." Josie inched to the edge of her seat. "Do you want me to stay?"

"Of course, I do." Charlie tried very hard not to look at her phone, but the pull was stronger than her desire not to. "We only just got here," she tried.

"How about this." Josie rose. "I'll leave anyway so you can give all your attention to whoever is sending you those messages."

In a panic, Charlie stood. Had she really been that rude? Or was Josie prone to overreacting? Either way, she was right to assume that this wasn't going anywhere if a single text from Ava undid Charlie so obviously. "My apologies."

"It's fine, Charlie. I get it. You probably have a ton of admirers."

Charlie chuckled inadvertently. Why did everyone presume that so easily? It was extra funny—or sad, depending on how she looked upon it—because it couldn't be further from the truth.

"I haven't—" Charlie started, but Josie was moving toward the gate in the fence already. Charlie hurried after her. "Let's at least say goodbye properly."

Josie turned around and pressed a quick kiss to her cheek. She arched her eyebrows, as though asking *is that properly enough?* "Bye, Charlie. See you at practice on Wednesday."

As the gate fell shut, Charlie retrieved her phone.

What's her percentage?

Charlie stood grinning like a fool in her back garden, although she really didn't have a lot of reason to.

CHAPTER TEN

Charlie toyed with Ava's copy of *Crying Rivers*, trying to come up with a suitable message to write. When Ava had started to read a passage from the book last weekend, she'd stopped her from continuing because, unless Ava was different from everyone else who had ever talked to her about that book, she knew exactly which sentence Ava was going to read.

Charlie prided herself on writing straight from the heart, but *Crying Rivers* was a breakup book that contained a lot of the hurt about Robin, the ex before Jo. In a twisted way, Charlie had ended up being grateful for the agony that came with that breakup, even though it hurt like a bitch at the time.

Her phone rang. It was Nick. Charlie was running very late for a dinner party he and Jason were throwing, and this was his second call. The only other invitee was Ava, who had messaged Charlie throughout the week, cajoling her about the dedication Charlie would write for her in the book. She'd sent texts saying *'That must be some letter you're writing for me, Charlie. What's with you hanging onto the book for so long? Or do you have ulterior motives?'*

These messages didn't help with Charlie's growing obsession with all things Ava Castaneda. Not trusting her ability to resist temptation, she'd compelled Nick into hosting an event where Charlie could return the book "safely." After all, they were all friends now.

Screw it. She wasn't going to produce anything

poignant but distant with Nick calling her every two minutes. She'd been thinking about it for a week and had come up empty—nice work for a writer.

She put the book in her bag, just in case seeing Ava inspired her on the spot. Otherwise, she'd hang on to it for a while longer.

Before leaving her house, she texted Nick to let him know she was on the way. She planned to use the drive to calm her nerves. The writers' room had been frantic with last-minute changes. Both Liz and Charlie had been forced to miss softball practice on Wednesday, something Charlie didn't mourn too much because it meant she didn't have to make awkward small talk with Josie.

But that was nothing compared to how *all* her thoughts connected back to Ava, and every last one seemed to have a glow about it. Charlie basked in the attention Ava bestowed on her. Not that they'd actually seen or called each other. No, they'd texted. And liked each other's Instagram photos. Things like that. Ava had uploaded a video of herself at the gym, and, during a rare quiet moment at work, Charlie had stared at it like an idiot, repeating the ten-second video endlessly and wondering how someone so gorgeous and successful could also be so witty, down-to-earth, and fun to be around.

Her life would have been much simpler if Ava had turned out to be a jaded Hollywood character, or a spoiled woman surrounded by assistants. But she wasn't. Via text, she mercilessly teased Charlie about her hang-ups on percentages, her reluctance to discuss *Crying Rivers*, and how her ass had looked in the bathing suit Ava had lent her—and had even snapped a picture of.

By the time she arrived at Nick and Jason's house, Charlie didn't have an ounce of calm left in her body— the drive hadn't worked the way she'd wanted it to. And when Ava kissed her on the cheeks and threw an arm around her in a quick embrace, Charlie's blood flooded with lust again.

"What a week," she said, and plonked down on a chair in what used to be her happy place—Nick and Jason's garden—but was now taken over by Ava's presence.

Charlie had worked late in the writers' room and was wearing her usual casual clothes. Ava, on the other hand, was all dressed up in high-waisted black pants with a black blouse tucked in, accentuating her model waistline. Charlie would need more than one glass of wine before she'd feel less frumpy and annoyed with her choice of clothes. Nick and Jason somehow always managed to look as though their outfits had just come back from the dry-cleaners.

"May I pour you a beverage, madam?" Nick asked. He seemed to be in a good mood.

"A large one, darling," Charlie replied. Already, she couldn't keep her eyes off Ava, who sat opposite her.

While Nick and Jason occupied themselves inside with fetching drinks and preparing dinner, Ava leaned over the table, and asked, "On a scale of zero to one hundred, how stressed are you?"

Charlie threw her head back and tried to massage her own shoulders. "A hundred and fifty," she said.

"You're the most melodramatic person I know, Charlie Cross." Ava sighed exaggeratedly and rose from her chair. "But let me show you how good a friend I am regardless." She moved behind Charlie and swatted her hands away.

Charlie only had on a flimsy T-shirt, and the contact of Ava's fingertips with her body—though filtered through fabric—only made her more tense.

"Good grief. Have you considered a professional massage therapist?" Ava asked. She sounded genuinely concerned. "Your muscles are hard as a rock." She dug her fingers into Charlie's shoulders.

For the briefest moments, Charlie considered actually enjoying Ava's touch, but her protective instinct took over. Ava massaging her could only lead to more anguish. When her fingers brushed the bare skin of her neck, pangs of electricity coursed through Charlie. She covered Ava's hand with her own and patted. "I'm sure you can recommend someone." Ava stopped working her fingers into Charlie's flesh. "But for now, why don't you sit back down, please?"

Their hands remained in place for a second longer, lingering, neither one of them displaying much desire to change the situation, until Charlie removed hers.

Ava gave her shoulders one last squeeze, and headed back to her chair. "Sorry. Did that make you uncomfortable?"

"Somewhat," Charlie said, unable to look Ava in the eyes.

Luckily, Nick darted back out with a tray of finger food and a glass of wine for Charlie.

"That looks scrumptious," Ava said.

"Help yourself, please." Nick joined them at the table and sucked most of the sexual tension between Charlie and Ava out of the air. Although, when Ava licked her fingers after having devoured an asparagus-and-pancetta roll, the sight instantly connected with something deep in Charlie's belly. She should go for a run tomorrow, or a hike. Either way, she needed to do *something* to alleviate the growing tension in her body.

After all four of them had gathered around the table for a simple but delicious plate of burratta dressed with tomatoes and the smoothest olive oil, Charlie made her announcement.

"I'm going to be auctioned off for charity."

"Say what now?" Nick said.

Charlie explained about the singles' auction the

softball league had scheduled to take place in two weeks.

"If it wasn't for a good cause, I'd find it quite crass," Jason said.

"I do wonder how much you'll go for," Nick said. "And are you going to have any stipulations read out before they start, erm, offering you for sale? Like, anyone less than a hundred percent needn't apply?"

"Leave her alone, Nickie," Ava said quickly. "I think it's very admirable."

While Nick uttered an offended "Ooh," Charlie looked at Ava. If she was going to start being chivalrous as well now, Charlie might have to refrain from spending time with her at all.

Ava shot her a wink, then continued to sop up olive oil off her plate with a hunk of bread. No low-carb diet for Ava either.

"Have you seen Jo?" Charlie suddenly heard herself ask Jason. She didn't really know why she was inquiring about her ex's whereabouts. Despite Jo coming to LA, Charlie hadn't thought about her all that much lately. Perhaps she needed a change of subject.

Jason nodded. "She's staying at The Standard on Sunset and will be there for a few more days. She took the job."

"Oh."

"Do you want to meet up with her?" Jason asked. "She has inquired…"

"Maybe. I'll see." Charlie put her fork down. "When is she relocating?"

"From what I hear, as soon as possible. The client wants to get started right away. But she has some things to sort out in New York first."

"Of course." Charlie nodded absentmindedly.

"You're taking this very graciously, Charlotte," Nick said. "You've grown as a person."

"You were right, I guess. It has been ten months

now."

"And not to worry, Christian will stay in New York."

"He'd better take good care of Stella and Fritzie."

"The children, erm, I mean cats," Nick explained to Ava.

Charlie slapped Nick playfully on the back of the head.

Nick ignored her and continued, "They'll commute back and forth every other week or so."

Charlie decided to postpone the long-awaited confrontation with her ex a little while longer. Odds were, Jo would spend a considerable amount of time with Nick and Jason. That meant she needed to make some sort of peace, because, arranged or not, they would see each other again soon.

The rest of the night's conversation meandered through a variety of easy topics, and Charlie started to feel almost fully relaxed in Ava's company as midnight approached.

They brought the used dessert dishes to the kitchen together, insisting that Nick and Jason stay put at the table.

After they'd deposited the crockery on the counter, Ava leaned against it and regarded Charlie. She looked so regal, and even taller than normal in those slacks.

"So?" she asked.

"So... what?"

"My signed copy of *Crying Rivers*?" Ava grinned.

"Oh, right. I'm sorry, I haven't been able to come up with something suitable yet."

"Should I take that as a compliment?" Ava cocked her head.

"Definitely."

"Well, then I insist you hand deliver it to my house later this weekend."

The words *Not safe! Not safe!* flashed in Charlie's brain. "Okay," she said, bypassing her gut instinct. "I'll bring my own bathing suit this time, just in case."

"Pity. I was hoping to put a slinky tiger print number on you." Ava smiled and Charlie melted all over again.

"Not a chance." Charlie wanted to stay in this almost tender moment of flirtation for the rest of the weekend, but Ava pushed herself away from the counter. Wordlessly, they headed back out.

After they said their goodbyes—which included a loose hug that lingered a few moments longer than politeness required—Charlie went home and tortured herself some more by watching *Knives Out* videos on YouTube.

CHAPTER ELEVEN

After Sunday's softball game, Charlie skipped post-game drinks, and declined an invitation from Liz and Sarah to join them for dinner with a few friends at their house.

Fully aware of her one-track mind, Charlie drove to Malibu, determined to somehow hash out this ever-growing attraction to Ava, without actually acting on it.

When she rang Ava's bell, though, it took several minutes—long enough for Charlie to worry—before Ava opened the door. When she finally did, Ava's lips were drawn in a thin line and the whites of her eyes were dotted with tiny burst veins.

"Are you all right?" Charlie asked.

Ava just stood there and looked at Charlie. "Not according to some people."

"Erm, can I come in?"

"Oh, yes, of course." Ava moved to the side and closed the door behind Charlie. No hello kisses or embraces were exchanged.

"What's wrong?"

"I had brunch with my so-called friend Eric and he gave me a piece of his mind." Ava marched through the house. "Do you want a sherry?" With a snap of her wrist she opened the liquor cabinet in the living room.

Charlie figured she had enough time to sober up before heading back home, and it was always better to drink with a friend when distressed. "Sure." Ava deposited the sherry glasses on the table with two resolute bangs.

"Why don't I pour?" Charlie asked. "You sit down."

"Gosh, I'm sorry, Charlie. Where are my manners?" Ava set the bottle on the table with noticeably less force. "I haven't even properly said hello. Come here." Ava opened her arms wide.

Charlie curved her arms around Ava's waist.

"I'm so happy to see you," Ava whispered in her ear.

This was not how mere friends greeted each other, but she still replied, "Me too." When they broke from their hug, they stared at each other for a brief moment until Charlie broke the connection. "Right. Sherry." She poured them both a small amount and they headed outside.

As soon as they sat, Ava knocked hers back.

"What happened?" Charlie asked, fiddling with the tiny sherry glass. Sherry wasn't her favorite drink.

"I don't know where to begin without sounding like a rambling woman." Ava took a deep breath. "Earlier at Nosh, Eric, out of the blue, started flirting with me. I called him out on it and, in the process, also informed him that I'm interested in someone else. He is one of my best friends, after all. I should be able to tell him things like that."

An unwelcome tingle sprouted in Charlie's stomach. She pushed her glass of sherry in Ava's direction.

"He asked who, of course, and I told him about my feelings for you." Ava was so matter-of-fact about this, Charlie was glad she was sort of rambling because she wasn't able to add to the conversation. Her brain needed to process first. Ava continued, "He nearly went ballistic. He was probably jealous, but still, that's no excuse to talk to me that way."

"What did he say?" Charlie hoped she was doing a good job of masking her emotions.

"That I must be going through menopause and stupid bullshit like that. Really nothing worth repeating. I… feel so betrayed by him. Like our friendship means nothing because he suddenly decided he still has feelings for me. After five years! I mean, I know what it's like to be single and all that. I know it's not pleasant sometimes, but come on… Have some self-respect."

"Has he apologized?" Charlie had no clue what else to say. Wasn't she toying with Ava's feelings just as much?

"I didn't give him a chance. I stormed off. He's been calling and texting but I put my phone on silent."

"Friends can be assholes sometimes. Nobody's perfect, right?" Charlie eyed the sherry she had shoved away. She kind of wanted it back now. "I'm sure he feels awful."

"I hope he feels that way for a long time." Ava reached for the second sherry and knocked it back as well. "I'm sorry for being such a drama queen today, Charlie. Emotions have been running a bit high of late."

"You really don't need to apologize to me."

"He did ask one very pertinent question, though." Ava's gaze flicked from Charlie to some undefined point behind her. "Why can't I have you, Charlie? If I'm so crazy about you, why can't we be together?"

"I think we need another drink." Charlie went inside to fetch the bottle of sherry. She used the time to inhale deeply a few times.

"It's okay," Ava said as soon as Charlie returned with the bottle. "I know why you don't want to be with me. No need to explain again."

This made Charlie feel like an idiot. She refilled the glasses. Ava downed hers immediately again.

"Do you want to swim?" she asked, her words slurring.

"I presume these are not your first drinks of the

day?" Charlie examined Ava's face closely. Her eyes drooped and the corners of her mouth curved downward.

"I was at brunch, remember?"

"I'm going to make some coffee." Charlie didn't wait for a reply and ventured back inside. Ava had a fancy, professional-looking coffee maker, and it took Charlie a while to figure out how everything worked. In the end, she managed to brew a large mug for each of them. When she gave Ava her coffee ten minutes later, the level of the sherry bottle had gone down farther.

"Drink this," she instructed, moving the bottle to the other end of the table.

Ava obeyed.

Part of Charlie wanted to flee this situation and the conversation they needed to have, but she couldn't leave Ava like this.

After a few more sips of coffee, Ava's eyes lit up. "Did you bring the book?"

"Yes." Charlie curved her fingers around the warm mug.

"Can I see it?" Ava raised her eyebrows.

"It's yours, so yes, although I'm not sure you're in the right state for it." Charlie didn't reach for her bag.

Ava banged her elbows on the table. "Not to worry, Charlie, my moment of melodrama is passing quickly." She let her head hang for a few seconds, her long hair obscuring everything but her shoulders. Then, with a quick movement, she flicked her head back, hair and all. "I'm my old self again." She finished with a wide smile.

A chuckle rose all the way from Charlie's belly. "Fine." She dug the book out of her bag—which also held a swimming suit—and slid it in Ava's direction.

Ava clutched the book to her chest. "My treasure." She found Charlie's eyes. "The other week when I wanted to read from it, why didn't you let me?"

Charlie decided there was still a good amount of

alcohol clouding Ava's brain. "Because I can't bear it when people say my words out loud. I can't really explain it, but it embarrasses the hell out of me. Especially the line you were about to read."

"How did you know which one I had picked?" Ava started thumbing through the book. "Are you brilliant *and* psychic?"

"Neither, but people can be quite predictable."

"Really? So you knew I was going to read this one." Ava opened the book. She opened her mouth, took a deep breath, then said, "I'm just teasing you, Charlie. I don't know why, but I seem to derive great pleasure from doing so." She smiled warmly. "Can I read your dedication or would you rather I wait?"

A sweat broke on her back, but she nodded. "Go ahead. But don't read it out loud." Charlie had spent the better part of her Saturday trying to come up with something—again. She'd finally settled on:

To Ava,
May our new friendship inspire many stories, all of them with happy endings.

"That's so sweet. Thank you." She paused. "Do you have time to work on a new novel now that you're doing *Underground*?"

It was a friendly enough question, and much more poignant than Ava could possibly realize, because, as much as Charlie enjoyed the experience of bringing *Underground* to the screen, she didn't have enough free time to devote to other writing.

Charlie dabbed her brow. She was hit with the sudden realization that what they were trying to do was madness. Every conversation they shared made her feel closer to Ava, strengthening feelings she wouldn't allow herself to act upon. She couldn't even imagine confiding in Ava about how much she missed actual ass-in-chair solitary writing. Nor could she casually tell Ava about anything else going on in her life. "I'm sorry. I can't do this. I can't sit here and chit-chat with you. It's driving me insane." Charlie sighed. "I have serious feelings for you, and they're not going to disappear if we continue to be 'friends.' Who are we kidding?"

Ava put the book down, her fingers tracing the lines of the cover image. "Then what do you suggest?"

Saying the words felt like someone was piercing a stake through her heart. "I think we shouldn't see each other for a while. Let things cool down a bit."

"That's the last thing I want to do." Ava combed her perfectly sculpted eyebrow with a fingertip. "Tell me honestly, Charlie, are you ever going to be able to give me a fair chance?"

"I don't know." Charlie scratched her cheek to give her hand something to do. "I want to, so very much, but I'm afraid that if I do, I'll screw things up even more."

"How, though? How can it be worse than it is now? Clearly, we can't be friends. So why don't we just try?"

To convince herself more than anything else, Charlie shook her head. "I wish it could be that simple."

"What if it is? What if you're so stuck inside the mess in your head you're not allowing it to be?"

Charlie shook her head more vigorously. "It's all fresh and exciting now. And yes, it would be simple and easy to date, fall into bed, fall in love, but what happens when you get tired of me? When the newness wears off and you realize you confused falling in love with me with something else?"

"Any new relationship has so many ifs, Charlie. There's always a risk. It doesn't mean you shouldn't try. If you stop trying, you might as well give up on love altogether."

"I will happily try as soon as the right person comes

along."

"Ah." Ava tapped a fingertip on the tabletop. "Like Josie, you mean?"

Charlie narrowed her eyes and tried to ignore the rising feeling of dread in her stomach. "I understand your sarcasm, I really do. But you have no idea how hard I had to struggle to get back on my feet after Jo left me. I'd be a fool to not do what I can to prevent that from happening again."

"Newsflash, Charlie. I'm not Jo."

"I know. At least Jo identified as a lesbian when we met, not that I cared much back then." Charlie felt the push of tears behind her eyes.

"Doesn't that totally disprove your theory?"

"We can theorize all we want. It won't change how I feel."

"Even if that makes you a coward who's willing to sacrifice something potentially beautiful just so you can continue to be miserable on your own?"

"You're forty-five years old, Ava. Don't you think you would know by now if you had any real attraction to women? Sleeping with a few female friends along the way just makes you a cliché."

"Okay. Time-out. Please."

Charlie drew some air into her lungs, but continued despite Ava's request for a reprieve. "Don't you think I want to be different? I hate feeling like this. It's hell to have this huge crush on you, to get to know you better and discover that you might very well be one of the greatest people I have ever met. But I just can't act on it. Giving in to you would set off so many alarms in my brain, we'd be doomed from the start."

"Well, then I guess your solution is the only one we have." Ava's usually straight posture slumped. "But, for the record, it doesn't have to be that way."

"I know it's my fault." Charlie wanted to get up, but

her legs felt like jelly. "If only…" she started to say, then thought better of it.

"If only what?" Ava was even attractive when she scowled like that.

"If only you'd, I don't know, actually fallen in love with Sandra. Or any other woman. Ever."

"I really like you." Ava's voice was small.

Although it was a flattering thing to hear, it only deepened Charlie's sorrow, because it further proved her point. "Yeah," she said. "It's not enough."

"I know." Ava's voice cracked.

Charlie had to go now. She hadn't touched the sherry, so at least that wouldn't affect her ability to drive. She finally rose. "I'd better go."

Ava nodded. Her body slumped in defeat. "It was nice knowing you, Charlie Cross."

Charlie hurried inside the house, and then out the front door, tears prickling in her eyes. When she reached her car, she gave the front tire a good kick. She steadied herself by planting both hands on the roof until the tears subsided.

Oh, how she wanted for Ava to come rushing out of that door she had just walked out of, hug her violently, and make her see what an awful mistake she was making. But Charlie's earlier words had not been spoken in vain.

It would never be enough.

CHAPTER TWELVE

During a break at work, Charlie killed time by scrolling through her Facebook feed. She didn't feel much like interacting with the others. She didn't feel like doing much of anything since she'd fled Ava's house last Sunday.

Her scrolling was interrupted by a message notification. It was from Liz, who was sitting two feet away from her at the other end of the table.

Will you ever smile again?

The message actually made Charlie smile and when she looked up at Liz, who was pulling a goofy face, Charlie genuinely laughed for the first time in days. Another message arrived on her phone, again from Liz.

Score!

"Come on." Liz got up and fixed her gaze on Charlie. "Let's get some fresh air."

Charlie let herself be dragged outside of the writers' room. "Even the weather never gets gloomy in LA," she said when they stood under the mild midday sun.

"If you're going to start complaining about too much sunshine, then I'm not sure even I, master of comedy, can save you."

"Since when are you a master of comedy?" Charlie

stared at Liz. "Tell me a joke right now, if you're such a comedic genius."

"I'm more a slapstick kind of person, Charlie. You know that. I'll be the first to admit I'm not very good at delivering the punchline to a joke." Liz brought her hands to Charlie's shoulders and squeezed tight. "Talk to me, buddy."

Charlie shrugged. "I blew it. I know I blew it. But even if I could go back in time, I don't know how I could undo my behavior. Not any of it."

Liz sighed and fixed Charlie with a determined stare. "You're scared, Charlie. Fear can make people behave like the biggest jerks."

"If only I knew how to stop being so afraid."

"I can't tell you that." Liz kept her hands on Charlie's shoulders. "But I can tell you this. There are never any guarantees in life. Jo might as well have left you for another woman instead of a man, but the point is that she left you. It's completely normal to be upset and hurt about that, but... I think you're focusing a little too much on *who* she's with now instead of *why* you're not together anymore."

"Maybe. I mean, yes, I know. And I wish I felt differently about this. I really do," Charlie said. "But I simply don't know how."

"Then you probably need some more time. Breakups are never easy." Liz finally let go of Charlie's shoulders. "Let me tell you something about Sarah and me. When we first met, I liked her immediately. I fell head over heels in love with her. All my thoughts were consumed by her and I wanted her bad. When we hooked up for the first time, I was over the moon. All my dreams were coming true and all that. But then, a day later, she told me she wasn't ready. She was still getting over someone else and it would be unfair to me to start dating again so quickly. She liked me very much and blah

blah blah, but she wasn't ready. And you know what? She was right." Liz fixed her big round eyes on Charlie. "Instead of moping around and taking it personally, I waited. Because she was worth it. We became friends first. Then we became closer and closer until, a few months later, she *was* ready. The rest is history." Liz wiggled the fingers of her left hand in front of Charlie, then pointed at her wedding ring. "What I'm trying to say is that things don't always work out the way you want them to, but they will work out if it's meant to be."

"Ava could surely have used a friend the other day after her brunch with Eric, but instead of being there for her, I ran away," Charlie said.

"Every situation is different. But yeah, you do have your head up your own ass way too much about this, in my humble opinion." Liz smirked. "But you know what else, Charlie? That's okay as well. You're obviously still hurting. And nobody can dictate how long your grief about a former relationship should last. Just take it easy and… try to start loving yourself a bit more again every day. You'll get there in the end."

"Do you mean I wallow in self-pity too much and chase gorgeous women away because of my self-loathing?" Charlie asked.

"What I mean, dear Charlie, is that you shouldn't be so hard on yourself, and that you shouldn't try to stick to a bunch of silly made-up rules in your head. That's all." Liz pulled up her shoulders. "Easy." She gave Charlie an encouraging smirk. "We should probably head back inside now." Liz put her arm around Charlie. "And don't forget, we all blow it sometimes. I'm sure even the divine Ava Castaneda has screwed up some things in her life. It's how you recover from your mistakes that matters most."

"You might not be a great comedian, but you're a wise woman, Liz. Sarah is so lucky that you waited for her." Charlie curved her arm around Liz's waist and they walked back into the writers' room like that.

"Glad you could join us, lovebirds," Michelle said, making the other writers break out in cat calls and wolf whistles.

"You're still up for the auction, aren't you?" Liz asked as she let go of Charlie.

"Anything for my dear friend Liz," Charlie said, and shot Liz a wink.

CHAPTER THIRTEEN

"For the life of me, I'm not missing a second of this lesbian auction," Nick said. "Jason, hurry up! We're late!"

Nick had lured Charlie into riding with them with the promise of not having to mind her alcohol intake, but he'd also instructed Charlie to arrive at least an hour before they had to leave so he could "correct her look." Charlie had arrived a half hour early, downed the better part of a bottle of wine, and swatted Nick's hands away whenever he made the slightest attempt to touch her. She knew far better than him what lesbians liked to see.

By the time they had to leave, and with a good amount of liquid courage in her system, she finally worked up the nerve to ask, "Have you seen Ava?"

"I see her on TV every week, darling," Nick said absentmindedly, a clear deflection.

"How is she?"

"Jason!" Nick yelled. "Jesus. Queens and bathrooms. It's a nightmare." He stopped pacing and sat down next to Charlie on the sofa. "Do you really want to know? I mean, you're not friends anymore. Maybe it's better to stop talking about her."

Charlie's work days had grown much longer now that *Underground* had started shooting and she had welcomed the opportunity to bury herself in work and the excitement of filming a TV show with both hands. Being near the one and only Elisa Fox didn't suck either. When she came home in the evening, she was too exhausted to even glance at her TV. Her YouTube binge watching had dramatically decreased as well. "Okay, Nickie, if you say so."

"For some reason, she has started seeing Eric again. It must be her way to forget about you, which I have told her in no uncertain terms, but women can be so stubborn sometimes," he blurted out. How long had he sat on this information, waiting for the right moment to share it?

The news still hit Charlie like a slap in the face. "She's seeing Eric again?"

"Apparently he made some big love declaration. I don't know too many details. Last time we spoke, she seemed kind of reluctant to address the topic."

Jason finally emerged from the bathroom, every single hair on his head in the exact spot it was meant to be in. "I'm ready," he exclaimed triumphantly, as though it were a major feat to only need an hour to groom himself.

"The car's been waiting for hours." Nick emphasized the word "hours," not exaggerating at all, as usual.

"You look smashing, Charlie. I bet you'll go for a million bucks."

Charlie had been so busy with work and trying not to think about Ava, she hadn't paid a lot of attention to the day of the singles' auction creeping closer.

"Let's go," Nick said. "Lesbians don't wait."

* * *

When they arrived at the venue, the place was heaving. As though she'd been waiting, Liz pounced on Charlie as soon as she saw her, barely noticing Nick and Jason.

"There you are," she said. To her credit, she didn't tap her watch. Liz was co-organizer of the auction. "I know this was all in the e-mail I sent you last week, but you'll need to come backstage at a quarter to nine exactly. You can be there sooner, but definitely not later, okay?"

"Who's this policewoman, Charlie?" Nick asked.

It seemed to finally register with Liz that Charlie had brought Nick Kent.

"Oh my God," she said, totally out of character. "I absolutely adore you." Then she slapped Charlie in the arm. "Why haven't you introduced us before? You know I love *Laughing Matters*."

"Erm, Lizzie, you told me you had applied for a writer job on the show years ago. You never actually said you loved it."

"Hi, I'm Nick's husband." Jason stepped forward, hand outstretched. "But I also go by Jason."

Liz, Nick, and Jason exchanged some niceties, and Charlie took the opportunity to scan the room. She spotted Josie and a few other members of her softball team to the left of the stage. Britt caught sight of her and waved, Charlie waved back.

"I have to go now," Liz said. "Please make sure Charlie does as she's told," she said to Nick and Jason. "And I do hope you'll stay for the party after. All proceeds go to the youth homeless shelter."

"Wouldn't miss it," Jason said, and patted her on the back. "You're awesome for organizing this."

"Check this." Nick handed Charlie a flyer as Liz sped off. "You're the top catch tonight, Charlotte."

Charlie took the paper from him. Liz had sent it to her for approval a few days ago. It was likely that the poor woman had barely gotten any sleep, what with the show filming at a hectic schedule and putting this fundraiser together. Seeing the picture of herself printed out like that gave Charlie a strange sensation in her stomach. Now that she'd seen the flyer, it was as if all eyes were on her.

"No seats?" Nick pouted. "Lesbians really have no

class."

An amplified tap-tap-tap came through the speakers. Charlie took the opportunity to shove Nick playfully in the shoulder. Then a woman Charlie didn't know took the stage and welcomed them all.

"I'll get us some drinks," Charlie offered. The presenter was still making introductions and giving details about the chosen charity. According to the flyer, ten women would be auctioned off tonight, and she was the last on the bill. She could either be nervous until it was her turn or drink away the knots coiling in her stomach. She chose the latter. She headed to the bar and purchased a bottle of red wine.

She said hello to Sarah and Tiff on the way back to the boys, then poured them generous portions.

"Take it easy, tiger," Nick said. "You don't want to fall off the stage. Think about your net worth for the next hour, please."

Megan, the first woman under the hammer belonged to a team Charlie hadn't played against yet, so she didn't know her. She'd scrutinized Liz's flyer and the only woman she'd been remotely tempted to make an offer on was Josie. It was probably a bad idea, but Charlie didn't dismiss it entirely just yet.

The crowd roared, and bidding paddles were thrust into the air generously. Megan went for $550 and was introduced to her date under loud cheers from the audience.

Charlie waited until Josie had disappeared backstage to say a temporary goodbye to Nick and Jason and join her teammates closer to the action.

Her team cheered exuberantly when it was Josie's turn. Sarah was the first to bid on her.

"Just to get the numbers up," she whispered in Charlie's ear.

Numbers soared for Josie and a quick-fire of bids

brought the sum to $1900 in no time.

"Should I bid?" Charlie asked Sarah.

Sarah widened her eyes. "For real?"

"I feel like I owe her."

While Charlie chatted with Sarah, two stubborn bidders pushed the amount higher and higher.

"Go for it," Sarah shouted. "Anything goes today!"

Charlie checked out her competition. The woman who had just bid $2400 was tall, blonde, and so LA Charlie believed she should stay out of this fight. The other person was Asian-American like Josie, but she was much bulkier and wore her hair shaved close to her head.

"It's now or never, Charlie." Sarah prodded her arm.

The MC acknowledged Charlie's raised hand and shouted, "We have a new contender in this race. That brings us to $3000, ladies and gentlemen."

The Asian woman scanned the room and, when she saw Charlie, shot her a filthy glare. Someone had the hots for Josie.

The blonde counter-offered, again.

"Three thousand one hundred," the MC said, her voice growing more high-pitched every time she screamed out a new amount. "Let's set a record here, folks."

Charlie raised her hand again. The blonde countered again, until they'd reached $3500, and Charlie's opponent resigned from the bidding war. Their teammates whistled and yelled encouragement to Josie, while slapping Charlie on the back.

Charlie was still coming down from the adrenalin rush of bidding, and only snapped out of it when the MC called her to the stage, as she had done with all the previous winners.

"Someone has deep pockets," the MC said. "We love that!"

"Some things have no price." Charlie stood next to Josie awkwardly.

"I know you're on the same team… literally and figuratively, so I won't introduce you. Enjoy your date, ladies."

Charlie and Josie left the stage together under loud applause.

"Seriously?" Josie asked as soon as they were backstage.

"Why not?" Charlie retorted. "I think we need a do-over. I know I screwed up last time."

"You guys." Liz headed in their direction, a big smile plastered on her face. "That was awesome!"

"We'll see about that later," Josie said.

"Oh, come on, this is for charity. Have some fun." Liz poked Josie in the bicep with her elbow.

Charlie cocked her head and fluttered her eyelashes, hoping to win Josie over with some slapstick.

"Okay, fine. I surrender. I will go on a date with you again. No phones allowed," Josie said.

"That's the spirit!" Liz beamed. "The next one's up. Charlie, no need for you to go back to the front now. It's almost your turn. You can watch from the side of the stage if you want. Or you can chat some more with Josie, of course."

"I'll gladly stay here," Charlie said. "I'm not entirely sure it's safe for me to go back out there. Someone gave me the evil eye just before I outbid her."

Josie lingered backstage with Charlie. "What happened to the woman who was texting you on our date?" she asked.

"She's out of the picture." It hurt for Charlie to say that, even though she smiled through it. "She's straight so—"

"Charlie, you're up!" Liz shouted.

"Good luck," Josie said, and gave her a thumbs up.

Charlie walked onto the stage and could barely see because of the spotlight that bathed the front of the house in a bright white light, and her eyes needed a moment to adjust.

Through the crowd's cheers, she could hear Nick's voice. It wouldn't surprise her if he bid just for laughs.

"Here we have Charlie Cross, ladies and ladies, and the five gents in the back!" the MC said. "Best get your check books out one last time."

Charlie had downed enough wine to not want to sink through the floor with mortification, but she wasn't feeling very natural and relaxed either.

"Do you need me to introduce the lovely Charlie or is that not required?" the MC asked the audience. They broke out in another cheer.

"Just get on with it," a low voice shouted from the back. Her team, positioned to the left side of the stage, hollered.

"As you wish," the MC said. "We can't possibly let Charlie Cross go for less than a thousand dollars, so let's start bidding at that price."

"One thousand five hundred," Nick shouted.

"Very well," the MC said. "Thank you, sir."

Charlie would die of embarrassment if no one bid higher than the gay friend she brought. It was nerve-wracking to be on display like that, like a piece of meat, being examined by hundreds of people.

To her relief, the bids kept coming. The league had advertised the auction well.

By the time the MC shouted "five thousand for the woman in red," most of the bidders had dropped out. Charlie's eyes had adjusted to the lights, and she was able to make out more and more of the faces in the audience.

"Does anyone bid more than five thousand," the MC asked.

"Six!" a woman in the middle of the pack shouted.

Charlie recognized her voice from earlier bids.

"Whoa!" the MC said. "This might be the winner right here!"

The crowd went silent with anticipation. Charlie's gut clenched.

Then, as the MC drew a breath to declare the last bidder the winner, a voice came all the way from the back.

"Ten thousand," the voice said. It was a voice Charlie would pick out of any crowd. She blinked a few times and shielded her eyes from the spotlight with her hand. All the way in the back, flanked by Nick and Jason, Ava stood with her hand raised defiantly—making a clear stand.

Charlie tried very hard to hold on to that feeling of pure joy that raced through her at the sight of Ava. For a fraction of a second, she felt like the luckiest girl on the planet.

"That definitely seals the deal," the MC, now almost completely beside herself, screamed. "While we give Charlie and her generous bidder a big round of applause, may I ask that the lady in the back come to the stage, please?"

The crowd cheered, half of them craning their necks to see who had made such an outrageous bid on Charlie. Charlie could hear some muffled sounds of surprise coming from the audience.

Still in the jubilant grasp of an adrenalin rush, Charlie staved off any worries about Ava exposing herself like that, about having bid on Josie, about anything other than this moment of bliss she found herself in.

The crowd parted for Ava as she strode to the stage as though she were on the catwalk. She didn't glance at anyone and kept her gaze solely focused on Charlie. Charlie's heart slammed furiously against her ribcage. She wanted to skip the date altogether and just take Ava home.

There on the stage, Charlie was, at last, free of the fear that had paralyzed her for months.

Liz rushed to the front of the stage and gallantly offered Ava a hand as she climbed the steps. When Ava turned to them, the crowd went wild. Charlie didn't dare look to her left where Josie stood.

"It's Ava Castaneda, ladies!" the MC hollered. "How amazing is that?"

Ava gave the audience a quick wave then walked from the other side of the MC to Charlie. The smile on her face connected directly with Charlie's soul. It was odd to have this realization in front of a bunch of strangers, her softball team, and under a scorching hot spotlight, but for Ava, Charlie would try. She would banish the fear, the insecurity, and the jealousy. She would let Ava in.

Ava leaned toward her and whispered, "There's nothing I wouldn't do to make you realize how serious I am about you." She grabbed Charlie's hand and squeezed. Charlie couldn't remember a moment in her life when she'd been happier.

CHAPTER FOURTEEN

Charlie and Ava sat in the back of Ava's car. After the excitement of the auction's grand finale had died down, they had gone backstage, and Ava had whisked Charlie out of the venue. Charlie had a million questions, but the one burning in her mind the most was, "What about Eric?"

"Big mistake," Ava said. "I was upset and I did something stupid."

Charlie was too elated to question Ava further on this topic. She didn't want to think about Eric Brunswick on this magic evening. Since leaving the stage, their hands had barely lost contact. Charlie was perfectly all right with never letting go of Ava again.

"How did you get Nick to not spill the beans?"

Ava was wearing a simple, figure-hugging black dress, and Charlie couldn't keep her eyes off her.

"Simple." Ava smiled cheekily. "I didn't tell him."

"But when did you arrive? I never saw you."

"I had someone on the inside who kept me up to speed and let me know when to make my entrance."

"I can't believe this." Charlie grinned goofily. "You do realize you just came out?"

"Came out of what? The closet?" Ava ran a fingernail over the palm of Charlie's hand. "I'm really not hung up on that, Charlie. I don't care about any of that. All I wanted was for you to understand how I feel about you."

"You've certainly done that." Another sort of tension rose in Charlie's gut.

The sound of Ava's phone ringing came from her purse. "Oh, for crying out loud. I'm going to turn this thing off." It had been ringing and buzzing and chiming since they'd gotten into the car. Ava dug her phone from her bag and quickly looked at the screen. "Sandra's having a fit, but she's going to have to wait."

"You know at least a hundred people posted pics of us on Instagram and Facebook," Charlie said.

"Good for them." Ava's smile faded as the conversation went on. She switched off her phone altogether and slipped it inside her purse. "Look, Charlie, what I did tonight might seem rash and not very thought through for someone who makes her living in the public eye." Her nail dug a bit deeper into Charlie's flesh. "But I've considered every angle of this for the better part of two weeks, and there wasn't a counter-argument that could persuade me not to do it. I hope you know why."

Deeply moved, Charlie nodded.

"Let me say it anyway." Ava wasn't done with grand romantic gestures yet. It was her night for it. "Because you're worth it, Charlie. Despite all that's holding you back in that tortured mind of yours, and your silly percentages, and how you've brushed me off several times now… I want you to give me a chance." She lifted Charlie's hand from her lap and brought it to her mouth to plant a kiss on one of Charlie's knuckles. "Give *us* a chance."

The kiss swept through Charlie the way a bolt of lightning hits a lone tree. It stripped her of every possible defense and left her bare.

"Besides," Ava continued. "I've read every word you've ever published, and I know all about your flair for the dramatic. A big gesture was required to make you snap out of your, frankly, morose state. I guess it worked." Ava kissed Charlie's knuckle again.

"Have you even paid for me yet?" Charlie joked, although she suspected that, if Ava didn't stop being so damn sexy, pretty soon her voice would lose all its power.

"Your friend made me sign something before we eloped."

"Liz." Charlie chuckled. "She should moonlight as an event organizer."

Charlie hadn't paid any attention to the road, and veered slightly to the left as the car took a sharp turn. Had they arrived at Ava's house already? Was she ready for this?

If she wasn't tonight, she never would be.

Once inside, Ava pulled Charlie to her instantly and, before kissing her, joked, "I paid a lot of money for this so you'd better make it worth my while."

This didn't help Charlie's growing nerves. "You paid for a date. I mean, if the woman in red had won, I wouldn't be about to kiss her right now, would I."

Ava tipped her head to the side and stared at Charlie with those dark eyes. "What are you saying, Charlie? You don't want to kiss me?"

"Hell no." Charlie couldn't wait any longer. She lifted her hands to the back of Ava's head and brought her lips to within an inch of Ava's. "Thank you," she said, before letting their mouths meet.

This kiss was different from the first one they'd shared on the beach because, instead of flooding Charlie with doubts, it shredded every last one she had. She'd been foolish to try to fight this attraction. Crazy to think she could get over Ava. Cowardly for surrendering to fear like that.

"I hope you're staying this time," Ava said when they broke from their kiss.

Charlie replied by kissing Ava again, and slipping her tongue inside. Ava's one hand was on her cheek, the other on her neck, and Charlie was starting to lose it a little already. Not only was her heart going mad inside her chest, but her quickened pulse had reached other body parts as well.

"Come on. You haven't been upstairs yet." Ava took hold of Charlie's hand, pulling it away from her grasp on Ava's neck.

Walking up the stairs of Ava's beach house, the events that were about to unfold very clear in her mind, was a surreal experience. Ava's behind danced against the tight fabric of her dress as they climbed to the first floor, and Charlie's breath hitched in her throat. She'd barely touched another woman since Jo. That kiss from Ava on the beach a few weeks ago was the most action Charlie'd had in many months. She couldn't even remember the last time she had made love. And now, Ava wanted her so badly she'd braved a crowd of rowdy lesbians to make that point. Charlie couldn't quite wrap her head around that yet. But she was doing this; she was going all in with Ava.

"You can admire my bedroom later," Ava said, and dragged her close for another kiss. "I've been dreaming of this for a long time, and I can't wait any longer." Her kiss was more insistent this time, her lips moving against Charlie's with more purpose. She trailed them to Charlie's ear and whispered, "I want you, Charlie Cross. Please get that through that thick skull of yours."

If there ever was a moment post-Jo that Charlie could easily push all her doubts and neurotic quirks to the side, this was it. Ava's breath hot in her ear, her hands already tugging at Charlie's tank top. She let her body slip into auto pilot, let it take control over her mind.

"Turn around," she said. Ava shot her a smile and spun on her heels.

Charlie unzipped Ava's dress. The flutter of nerves in her stomach was replaced by pure lust. She didn't need to be able to wrap her head around the fact that she was about to take Ava to bed to know exactly what to do.

It took a bit of ass wiggling to get Ava's dress to fall to the floor. Charlie's breath caught at the sight of Ava's back, naked except for the fine lace of her bra. She'd seen her in a bikini, but these circumstances were entirely different.

Ava didn't turn to face her. Instead, she brought her hands to her back and unclasped her bra. When she spun around, she held the fabric to her chest with both hands.

"Are you ready for this, Charlie?" she asked, her voice filled with teasing lust.

Charlie nodded. Ava didn't drop her bra. Instead, she grinned and said, "Oh, you thought I meant *this*?" She removed her bra a fraction of an inch away from her breasts. "Well, *I* meant for you to take off your clothes."

Charlie sank her teeth into her bottom lip and regarded Ava. "I want *you* to take them off."

They stood in a quiet, heavily charged stand-off for a split second, then Ava acquiesced. She let her bra drop to the floor. Charlie's sanity dropped with it, and all she wanted was to tear her own clothes to shreds that very second if it would get her any closer to pressing her naked body against Ava's.

"Very well, Charlie." Ava took a step closer. "But remember, you asked for this."

Ava brought her hands to Charlie's side and lifted up her tank top at a painfully slow pace. Charlie suppressed a groan.

Charlie stretched out her arms and, Ava being taller than her, she slid the shirt over her head easily. Next, she trailed one hand down Charlie's chest, all the way to the button of her jeans, and flipped it open.

"Jesus," Charlie moaned. Ava's hands on her, touching her like that, were about to make her spontaneously self-combust.

Ava cocked her head as if to say "You asked for this." Charlie let her get on with it without interfering. Ava brought her hand back up Charlie's torso, drew a circle around her belly button, then dragged a finger upward and traced the edges of Charlie's bra.

The expanse of Charlie's skin broke out in goose bumps, and her pussy lips throbbed beneath her jeans. Ava dipped a finger inside Charlie's bra and nearly brushed against her nipple.

Ava trailed her fingers along the length of her belly again and this time, she slid open Charlie's zipper. "Why don't you get out of these jeans." She took a step back, revealing her naked chest. Charlie's mouth dropped open and she forgot what she was supposed to be doing.

"Jeans only," Ava warned. "It's how you wanted it." She shrugged in an exaggerated fashion.

Charlie wobbled and almost fell over trying to heel off her shoes and get her pants off her legs in the same movement. Then she stood in front of Ava in just her underwear. Instinctively, and perhaps also because Ava had been bare chested for a while now, Charlie's hands traveled behind her back.

Ava clicked her tongue and wiggled a finger. Charlie dropped her hands to her side.

"Now." Ava stepped closer again. "I will finish undressing you, Charlie. But I will take my sweet time. After all, you made me wait for this long enough."

All the pent-up lust Charlie hadn't been able to release—because she hadn't even allowed herself a quick masturbation session to blur some of the images of Ava in her mind—overpowered her senses. Her chest rose and fell in rapid swells as her breath picked up speed. Her panties were drenched, and seeing Ava stretch an arm toward them wasn't helping.

As she had done with the edge of her bra cup earlier, Ava traced a finger along the waistband of

Charlie's panties.

"Nice undies, Charlie," she said, a tad of mockery in her voice. "Did you wear them especially because you were being auctioned off?"

Charlie couldn't reply—her brain had stopped functioning as soon as Ava's finger touched the skin of her belly. Ava maneuvered her hand between Charlie's legs and, with the lightest of touches, swept it along the soaked panel of Charlie's panties.

Charlie couldn't stifle the moan coming all the way from the bottom of her heart. "Oh God, Ava, please." If Ava kept this up, she'd come way too soon. Her exasperation didn't stop Ava. She located Charlie's clit and drew a circle around it.

Charlie huffed out a burst of air through her nose, trying to steel herself. "Please," she pleaded. "You don't understand."

"I don't understand what, Charlie?" Ava kept trailing loose, wide circles around Charlie's clit, her finger only separated from Charlie by a flimsy piece of soaked-through fabric. "What teasing feels like?" She nipped at Charlie's ear.

"If… you don't… stop…" was all Charlie managed to say. Tension built and built in her muscles. This was not how she wanted it. It wasn't a suitable climax for the night they'd shared so far.

Then, thankfully, Ava's hand retreated. She slipped her fingers in the waistband at the side and tugged Charlie's panties down. The rush of air on her puffed-up lips calmed Charlie down, but only a fraction. Clearly, her biggest task for the rest of the night would be keeping herself from reaching orgasm too soon.

"We need to take the pressure off you, Charlie." There was a hint of impatience in Ava's voice now. Seemingly fed up with slowly teasing Charlie, she undid the clasp of her bra, and threw it on the floor. "Sit on the bed."

Of all the things Charlie might have imagined in an unguarded moment, she'd never expected Ava to be this bossy. Charlie was the one with experience; she should be the one calling the shots. But she was too overwhelmed, too amped up, and just too damn horny to assert any dominance over Ava. All she managed was a quick defiant stare into Ava's eyes before she sat as commanded.

Ava stood before her with a wide grin on her face. "Let me show you once and for all, Charlie Cross, that a percentage is just a silly number." Ava kneeled before Charlie and kissed her thigh. Then, gently, she pushed Charlie's legs apart.

Charlie leaned back on her hands, and cool air rushed over her tortured sex. She looked down at Ava's mass of raven-black hair and admired the way it fanned out along her upper thighs. Ava's breath rushed over her pussy, making the air between her legs grow hotter

Charlie's skin flushed, her flesh over-heated, and her clit was ready to explode into a mind-numbing orgasm. She thought she might come just from having Ava lower her head between her legs. Then she stopped thinking altogether because Ava planted a kiss on her inner thigh, coaxing a low, breathy groan from Charlie.

As though Ava knew that waiting any longer was futile, her next kiss landed just below Charlie's clit. The next one followed even quicker and soon Ava was raining down soft kisses between her legs. Before long, Ava's tongue joined the action, and the moment it slid in the direction of her clit, Charlie was lost.

It only took a few flicks before Charlie brought one hand to Ava's hair and buried her fingers in the glossy, lush mane, while a climax shuddered through her and a guttural cry escaped her mouth. When Charlie's muscles relaxed, she let herself fall onto the bed and a tear slid out of the corner of her eye.

Ava hopped onto the bed and draped her warm body over Charlie's shivering flesh.

Charlie pulled Ava as close as she could, wanting to disappear in her for a moment.

"Jesus Christ," she muttered. "That was a long time coming."

Ava pushed herself up and looked down at Charlie. With the back of her hand, she stroked Charlie's cheek and brushed away the tear.

Everything that had held Charlie back from actually doing *this* dissolved when the tension finally drained from her body. She felt freer than she had in a year. Released from a curse she'd cast on herself. Now that her most urgent needs had been met, Charlie was ready to play her part.

"My turn," Charlie said, lightly tracing a fingertip over the skin of Ava's back. "Let's see how long you last."

Ava narrowed her eyes. "I'm not saying it's a contest, but if it were, you never stood a chance, Charlie dear."

That did it. Charlie pushed herself up from the mattress and toppled Ava off her. In no time, she had Ava on her back and she straddled her slender waist. Charlie grabbed Ava's wrists and pinned them above her head. "Time to wipe that triumphant grin off your lips," she said, although uttering these words had nothing to do with how she really felt inside. Beneath her skin, desire, infatuation, and the events of the night blended into a heady mix of pure ecstasy. Charlie was about to slip her fingers inside Ava. The woman she'd walked away from. The woman who had come after her, fought for her, and showed her that Charlie had better take her seriously.

Charlie released Ava's wrists and smiled down at her, staring into her eyes. Ava's lips parted in a grin, baring a perfect row of the whitest teeth. When she smiled like that, her cheeks creased and created the most adorable dimples.

She flanked Ava, barely touching her. It was high time to acquaint herself with the more intimate parts of Ava's gorgeous body.

Charlie let her fingers skate along Ava's belly, meandering upward, to the delicious curve of her breast. Despite just having experienced a freeing orgasm, arousal pulsed in her clit at the first contact with Ava's breast. She circled her fingers around Ava's dusky nipple, stiffening it into a delicious peak.

When Charlie looked at Ava's face, all smugness had drained from it and she lay with her eyes half-shut and her lips parted. Gently, Charlie took Ava's nipple between her fingertips and squeezed, luring a moan from Ava's lips. Ava dug her nails in Charlie's back. Charlie tightened her grip slightly, proud to wear any mark Ava left on her.

Charlie repeated the process on Ava's other nipple, bringing it to a hard knot under her touch. When she moved her hand lower, she brought her lips to Ava's nipple and sucked it into her mouth. Charlie's clit joined the pulsing party between her legs. If she had her way the bed wouldn't see a lot of sleeping that night.

"Oh, Charlie," Ava moaned. She threaded her fingers into Charlie's hair. Charlie released Ava's nipple and met her gaze. Ava said, "This is no time to exact revenge for me teasing you earlier. I've been waiting, too, remember?" Ava's voice was shot through with breathy lust.

Instead of teasing Ava the way Ava had done to her so cruelly earlier, Charlie slipped her hand inside Ava's panties, meeting nothing but wetness. Ava released Charlie's hair and grabbed Charlie's hand, guiding her farther into her panties.

Charlie lowered her mouth onto Ava's nipple again and nibbled on it with her teeth, while her hand explored Ava's wetness. She needed to see, though. She needed to see Ava's soaked pussy lips.

Charlie let Ava's breast slip from her mouth, slid her hand out of her panties, and pushed herself up. She tugged Ava's panties down her long legs and, finally, looked. She had a sudden, overwhelming urge to start licking and lose herself in Ava's pussy. But Charlie wanted something else even more. She wanted to gaze into her eyes and fuck her with her fingers until she came.

Charlie repositioned herself by Ava's side and couldn't resist taking those tiny, dark nipples in her mouth again. While she did, she slid a fingertip between Ava's slick folds, then up to circle her clit.

"Fuck me, Charlie," Ava demanded. She really was bossy. And apparently only had patience to tease others.

Just from skating along her lips a few times, Charlie's fingers were entirely coated in Ava's juices. Charlie couldn't wait any longer either. She wanted to do this as much as Ava wanted her to do it to her. Charlie's fingers drifted to Ava's entrance and, ever so slowly, Charlie slid two fingers into Ava's pussy. She forced herself to take her time, to allow each moment to form solidly in her memory.

Ava gasped for air. The hand resting loosely on Charlie's back stiffened, nails digging into Charlie's flesh.

Charlie reveled in the sensation of her fingers being enveloped by Ava's inner heat. Ava thrust her hips against Charlie's hand, demanding more, and her desire pooled in Charlie's palm.

"Aaah," Ava moaned. "Oh, Charlie. Oh, Charlie." She repeated the words like a mantra, as though she needed to hear herself say them to tip over that edge.

Charlie focused all her attention on Ava, and drank in the changing expression on her face, the way her eyelids fluttered, and her lips contracted into a pout, her head thrown back into the pillow—but the pulse in her own pussy was impossible to ignore completely. Heat traveled beneath Charlie's skin as her fingers explored and stroked Ava deeply.

Then, Ava's body jerked a couple of times, and she curled her fingers around Charlie's wrist.

"Oh, fuck." Ava exhaled a deep breath.

Charlie eased her fingers out of Ava, kissing her softly on the mouth. Ava's lips stretched into a wide smile that was also reflected in her eyes.

"That was not a bad start," Ava said, folding an arm around Charlie's neck.

Charlie fell onto her back next to Ava, whose arm rested in the hollow between her neck and the pillow. "When I woke up this morning, this was the last place I expected to be after the auction." For all Charlie knew, she might even have successfully avoided Ava for the rest of her days in LA.

"I take it you'll be staying tonight?" Ava joked.

"If it were up to me, I'd never leave this bed again."

"Are you saying you want me to handcuff you to it?" Ava pushed herself up and stared down at Charlie.

"I did notice a bit of bossy streak. We'll have to do something about that." A warm glow expanded in Charlie's chest.

Ava leaned over and pecked Charlie on the cheek. "We'll see," she said without an ounce of sincerity in her tone.

CHAPTER FIFTEEN

When Charlie opened her eyes, the first thing she saw was the ocean. Frothy waves crashed onto the shore. She squinted to locate the exact spot on the beach where Ava had pulled her close and kissed her the first time.

She rolled onto her back. Ava was still asleep, lying on her side, the sheets thrown off, chest exposed. The tranquility on her face stood in sharp contrast to the expressions Charlie had witnessed throughout the night. They hadn't slept much, and as she stretched, Charlie discovered delicious aches in her body she hadn't experienced for more than a year, perhaps longer.

She lay staring at Ava a while longer. She wanted to stay in Ava's house forever, without having to face the outside world.

"Hey." Ava opened her eyes and looked straight at Charlie.

Instantly, the warm glow invaded Charlie's body again. "Morning." Charlie planted a kiss on Ava's forehead.

"That's it?" Ava asked. "How stingy."

"Hey, you should be glad I'm still here."

"This from the woman who wanted me to chain her to my bed last night."

"I said no such—" Charlie realized too late that Ava was teasing her.

Ava let out a giggle, then asked, "What time is it?"

"I have no idea." Ava's bedroom smelled of sex. "I

also have no idea where my phone is. I'm inclined to not give a shit." Charlie had nothing planned for the day.

Ava lay in silence for a few minutes, then brought her hands to her head. "Sandra must have lost her mind by now. I need to check my messages at some point today, I'm afraid."

"Maybe later," Charlie said, and kissed Ava on the forehead again. "Let's take a shower first."

"There's an idea. See, I knew you had some brilliance in you." Ava curved her arms around Charlie's neck and pulled her in for a deep kiss.

* * *

After a shower that lasted much longer than any Charlie had ever taken before, they sat at the breakfast bar in the kitchen. Ava stared at her phone. She hadn't turned it on yet.

"Perhaps I did lose my mind a little last night." She reached for her coffee cup and sipped. "All your fault, by the way."

"Why don't I switch mine on first? Assess the damage, to take that first edge off." Charlie toyed with her phone.

"Sure." Ava pricked a piece of mango onto her fork.

Charlie pressed the *on* button and waited for her phone to come alive. As soon as the screen lit up, an avalanche of messages rolled in.

"Most are from my teammates," she assured Ava. "A few dozen are from Nick, of course." She scrolled through and didn't see anything too unexpected. "No links to TMZ yet." She shot Ava an encouraging smile.

"Okay. Here we go." The messages on Charlie's phone were nothing compared to the buzzing and beeping of Ava's when she switched it on. She put it next to her coffee mug and, for two full minutes, stared at it as though she was willing it to stop violating her peace of mind. "Sandra only left me fifteen messages. Oh, and Eric called, of course. About fifty other missed calls. And I know better than to open any social media accounts right now." Ava pushed her phone away and looked at Charlie. "It *is* Sunday."

Charlie gave a light chuckle. "True. But maybe give Sandra a call. Let her know that everything will be all right."

"I can tell her that all I want, she's not going to believe me. I mean, I pay her not to believe me, really."

"Realistically, what's the worst that can happen?" Charlie asked. "It's not as if you went on a date with Elisa Fox or anyone like that. It's just me."

"Just you." Ava sat musing, then locked her gaze on Charlie's. "If I call Sandra, she'll want to come over. Our day will be ruined."

"You have to tell her something. For all she knows, I cast a spell on you and kidnapped you or something."

This brought a small smile to Ava's face. A smile that was quickly erased by the buzzing sound of the intercom. "Speak of the devil. I bet that's Sandra." Ava slid off her stool and headed toward the security screen mounted on the wall near the fridge. She pressed a button and a Mustang Charlie recognized from when she'd come to dinner appeared on the screen. It wasn't Sandra. It was Eric.

"Oh, Christ." Ava sounded as though her eyes were about to roll out of her head. "This is just perfect." She inhaled deeply, widening her stance on the floor—perhaps for extra support. "What?" she said rudely into the intercom.

"Can I come in?" Eric's voice came through the speaker.

"Why?" Ava's voice was full of impatience, making Charlie wonder what had actually happened between them.

"Why?" Eric repeated. "Because I'm your friend, and we work together, and we need to talk."

Ava sighed deeply. "Fine. But no lectures, please." She pressed a few buttons before turning around. "I'd best put some more clothes on."

"Do you want me to go?" Charlie asked, not excited to witness any of this.

"No, absolutely not." Ava walked toward her. "We have nothing to be ashamed of. If Eric wants to come in here and display his testosterone levels a bit, that's his business. I know exactly what he's going to say, because he has said it to me several times already." Ava planted a kiss on Charlie's forehead. "Could you please let him in while I at least put on a pair of pants?"

"Erm, I'm not exactly dressed either." Charlie was sitting on her stool in last night's tank top and a skimpy pair of underwear she'd borrowed from Ava.

"Right." Ava easily managed one of her wide smiles. "Then we have no choice but to let him stew for a few minutes. Come on."

They rushed up the stairs and Charlie had to search Ava's bedroom a few seconds to find her jeans. In the time it took her to recover and put on her bra, Ava had somehow magically transformed herself into a cover girl. Charlie had some questions about how she did that, but there was something she wanted to know even more.

"Did you and Eric part on, erm, amicable terms?"

"I wouldn't quite call it that." Ava smoothed a crease out of her blouse. "So best not let him wait too long."

They dashed back downstairs, and Ava let Eric in.

"We meet again," he said when he noticed Charlie lingering in the kitchen.

"Hi, Eric." Charlie hadn't engaged in too much direct conversation with Eric at the dinner party, but he'd come across as a pleasant enough guy.

Eric shook his head at her. "What were you even thinking, Ava? You can't just, just…" He seemed unable to find the words to describe the heinous act Ava had committed. "Just do what you did. I hate to be the one to say it, but you can't be that selfish. Not someone in your position. Not when other people's jobs are at stake."

"Please tell me how exactly I've put people's employment on the line?" Ava appeared calm in the face of Eric's madness.

"Are you kidding me?" Eric was a tall, fit man of about fifty, with a full head of gray hair. He wasn't exactly attractive, but what did Charlie know? So often women melted into puddles for men she thought looked ghastly. "We have an image to uphold. We owe that to the show."

"Oh, really? And what kind of image is that? The kind where the female host only has affairs with one of the male judges?"

Eric looked away from Ava and evaluated Charlie. He looked as if he couldn't quite believe he had to compete with the likes of her.

"I thought you knew better."

"Why don't you say what you've really come to say, Eric?" Ava fixed him with a cold stare. "Ted, your co-judge, is openly gay, for heaven's sake. This has nothing to do with the show, and we both know it."

"Well, you said it. Ted is gay. Has been for years. You, on the other hand…"

Charlie didn't have to imagine what jealousy looked like. She had a front row seat to The Big Jealousy Show right here and now.

Ava's features softened, and her voice was much mellower when she spoke next. "Let's both calm down, okay? I realize you must be hurt."

"Hurt?" Eric obviously wasn't ready to calm down. "Have you even been on the internet today?"

Ava expelled some air, then held up two fingers. "You have two choices, Eric. Either you sit, have some coffee, and take a deep breath. Or you leave right now."

Hearing Ava raise her voice like that made Charlie's heart beat faster. It was inappropriate given the situation, but she couldn't help herself. Bossy Ava turned her on.

Eric held up his hands in surrender. "Fine."

An apology would be nice, Charlie wanted to say, but thought it wasn't the best time for such a remark. She supposed she could see why he believed Ava with him made more sense than Ava with Charlie.

Eric sat, leaving one stool between himself and Charlie. Ava stood behind the breakfast bar and poured coffee.

"I don't mean to be rude, but could we perhaps talk privately?" he asked, looking directly at Ava, pretending Charlie wasn't there. "We have a history, Ava. I don't want to lay it all out in front of someone who has no business with... us."

Ava did roll her eyes now. "I don't know what you thought you could accomplish by coming here, but, so far, you've only managed to deeply offend me. Keep saying things like that and there will be more at stake than *Knives Out.*"

Charlie couldn't see Eric's face—and she was indeed starting to feel like the third wheel—but she did notice how his posture stiffened.

"I'm just trying to understand, Ava." He lowered his voice to a whisper, but Charlie had no trouble hearing. "Only last weekend, I believed you and I were getting back together, and now... this."

His words jarred Charlie. She and Ava hadn't had time to talk about anything. And now this man was sitting in Ava's kitchen, literally positioned between them. She'd been able to easily push back her fears of Ava leaving her for a man because of Ava's grand gesture and the mind-blowing night they'd shared, but that ability was starting to crumble. Ava and Eric could have shared exactly the same sort of night. No wonder the guy looked so utterly distraught.

"I should probably go," she said, now that her instincts were working again. Charlie pushed herself away from the counter. "Let you guys talk."

Eric visibly relaxed, while Ava's posture tightened. "No, Charlie. No," she said.

"I have some stuff of my own to deal with, anyway." A familiar flood of anxiety washed over Charlie. She tried to breathe her way through it, tried to reason with herself, but the sight of Eric, who was now facing Charlie fully, some kind of sparkle in his eye that hadn't been there before, was enough to make her flee.

Charlie fished her phone off the counter. Did she have a bag somewhere? She must have. Her keys weren't in her pocket. She also didn't have her car.

"I'm serious, Charlie." Ava walked over to her and put an arm around her shoulder. "I need you to stay." Her gesture wiped that sparkle right out of Eric's eyes. "If anyone should go, it should be Eric."

Eric arched up his eyebrows as if to say "Really?"

"You owe me more than a tepid cup of coffee, Ava. And you know it." With that, he slipped off the stool and, with his wide, loud manliness, bristled out of the kitchen and then out of the house.

As soon as he'd left, Ava sagged against a kitchen counter. "Way to kill the romantic vibe. I'm sorry about that, Charlie. That was not part of my plan."

Eric's arrival had set off several warning signals in Charlie's sex-sedated mind. Obviously, Eric had feelings for Ava. A position Charlie could easily understand and sympathize with.

"What happened last weekend?" There was a good chance the answer would ruin the very last of the romantic atmosphere, but Charlie had to know.

"A moment of weakness." Briefly, Ava covered her face with both her hands, as though trying to rub something away. "A huge mistake."

"Did you, huh, sleep with him?" Charlie's stomach rumbled with nerves.

"Does it even matter, Charlie? I mean, you didn't want to see me anymore."

"So you slept with Eric?" That old nagging feeling was chipping away at Charlie's common sense and she couldn't stop it.

"If you're going to start comparing... I urge you to remember that I had someone at the auction last night who kept me up to speed about *everything*."

Charlie appeared to be suffering from selective memory. Everything that had happened before Ava had made her phenomenal final bid seemed erased from her mind. But, of course she remembered making her own winning bid on Josie, the fraught conversation they'd shared backstage, and how that had given way to careful banter. In Charlie's mind, that in no way compared to sleeping with a man, but she had to keep her cool about this.

"What are you going to do about that, by the way?" Ava's hands were on her hips matron-style. "When are you going on your thirty-five-hundred-dollar date, Charlie?"

"I'm sorry. Point taken." Charlie did her best to control her fears, but deep down, the thought of Eric and Ava reuniting didn't sit right with her. Now that Eric had come breezing into Ava's house, flexing his muscles, Charlie couldn't get the image out of her head. Eric looking at Ava the way she had last night. The same images that had inundated her brain for months after Jo had left her for Christian. Even though she was standing in Ava's kitchen after a night of unbelievable passion, suddenly she could very clearly remember the reason why she had run away in the first place.

"We should make the most of today. Next weekend I'm going on location to Texas for the show. I'll be gone a few weeks," Ava said.

Charlie tried to ignore the cold fist that wrapped itself around her heart. "Next weekend?" she asked, not able to keep insecurity from seeping into her tone. "With Eric?"

Ava closed her eyes briefly, making it seem to Charlie that she couldn't believe the kind of love politics she had gotten herself into. "Yes, Charlie. He's part of the show. So are a hundred other people."

Charlie had the choice. She could be reasonable and give Ava the benefit of the doubt. She drew from the mindfulness exercises her therapist back in New York had taught her. *Count your breaths. Think before you speak. Don't say something you can't take back.* So Charlie counted to ten while breathing in and out. Ava, in all respects, was way out of her league, but nonetheless, had made a move Charlie couldn't possibly ignore.

"Are you going to say something?" Ava asked. "I believe I've made my position clear. I'm not going to keep on begging you to be with me."

Charlie nodded. "If you're going away next weekend, I'd better spend every waking moment with you until you get on that plane."

Ava smiled wide. "You had me worried there for a second. I thought you were going all neurotic on me again."

You have no idea, Charlie thought, while she walked into Ava's embrace.

CHAPTER SIXTEEN

"Do you own a strap-on?" Ava asked. They were lying in Charlie's bed in West Hollywood. Ava had invited herself over for their last night together before flying off.

"Not at present. No," Charlie replied, her stomach already aflutter. "I had one in New York. I have no idea what my ex did with it." Charlie assumed Jo probably burned it.

"Oh." Ava lay on her side, her hands tucked between her thighs. They were both naked.

"Why?" Charlie ran her hand over the back of Ava's arm. Was that disappointment lurking in Ava's voice?

"I just thought it would have been a nice farewell gift…" Ava curled her lips into a smile.

"For you to fuck me with?" After Ava had displayed that bossy streak in the bedroom during their first night together, Charlie was no longer under any illusions about who was the natural top in their relationship. Ava had all but tied her up. Charlie had no issues complying with any of Ava's requests, although in bed with Jo, she'd usually been the one to strap it on.

"I was thinking more of the other way around." Ava surprised her.

"Really?" Charlie asked.

"Is that so surprising?" Ava slipped her hands from between her thighs and caught Charlie's with hers.

Charlie jutted out her bottom lip. "A little, I guess."

"Why?" There was a chuckle in Ava's voice.

"I don't know. It's hard to explain. That's just how it feels when I'm with you."

Ava pushed herself up and rested her head on an upturned palm. "I wish you *could* explain. Will you try? For me?"

"See." Charlie chuckled. "You thirty-five percenters don't know anything."

"I thought we had established I'd gone up to around fifty by now." Ava put some mock-indignation in her tone.

As a joke over dinner last Sunday, they decided that Ava would go up one percentage point every time one of them reached orgasm. That was five days ago. While it was all well and good to tease, it didn't entirely chase the doubts from Charlie's brain. If anything, the fact that they had a running joke about it was telling enough.

Ava brought her fingers to Charlie's belly and let them hover over her skin. "I also didn't say I would *not* use it on you, Charlie. Don't worry. I know what you want."

Charlie felt like she'd had a personality transplant since sleeping with Ava. Not only had she had to come to terms with the fact that, yes, Ava had slept with Eric, and that they would be in Texas under the same circumstances that had brought them together the first time. Also, for Ava, Charlie turned out to be a total bottom. And she liked it. She didn't want it any other way. More than anything though, Charlie hadn't had enough alone time to obsess too much over her usual hang-ups.

When she wasn't on set, she'd been at Ava's—completely ignoring softball practice. She had three-and-a-half weeks to practice while Ava was filming on location. Liz, however, had expressed doubts about Charlie's investment in the team.

"Then why do you want me to use it on you?"

Charlie asked.

Ava continued to hold her fingers close to Charlie's stomach without touching and Charlie's clit strained wildly between her legs. A moment later, Ava let her fingers meet Charlie's skin. She also shook her head. "Oh, Charlie. Why do you always need twenty reasons for everything? You got out of it easy earlier by cracking a joke, but don't you think I know why you're asking me all of this? You are so unbelievably transparent." Ava's finger danced around Charlie's belly button. "Don't you want to stop thinking for once? Just go with the flow and, I don't know, try to trust me?"

Charlie started to say something in her defense, but Ava wasn't done with her speech yet.

"I want you to fuck me with a strap-on because it would be a new experience for me, and I'm always up to trying something new." Ava's hand curved up the slope of Charlie's breast. "Not because I need to be fucked with something that looks and feels like a penis before I go away for a month." With that, Ava caught Charlie's nipple between two fingers and squeezed too hard to be sexy. "You are so focused on one thing only, Charlie, I can read you like an open book."

"Ouch," Charlie yelped. It wasn't Ava pinching her nipple that hurt the most.

"Sometimes, you radiate fear," Ava said, while moving on to Charlie's other nipple. "It's not your most attractive quality."

This comment made Charlie want to shrink away from Ava's touch, curl up in a ball, and wallow in self-pity. But she really had nothing to feel sorry about, considering the fact that Ava was presently pinching her nipples.

"Maybe I'll visit you in Texas and bring you a present." Charlie wished she had a strap-on in the house right now.

"Please do." Ava's hand made its way down again. "But, until then, we'll have to make do with this." Her fingers skated along Charlie's pubic hair. "It's as though your level of arousal is proportional to how paranoid you are, Charlie. I'm beginning to think this jealous streak of yours is more like a fetish." Ava slipped her fingers between Charlie's wet folds, and she twisted them deep inside her.

"Fuck," Charlie moaned.

"You can say that again." Ava's face contorted with concentration, before she looked away from Charlie and shuffled lower, all the while keeping her fingers busy inside of Charlie. She didn't start easy with a few lighter thrusts, but fucked her as though demanding something urgent.

As soon as Ava brought her tongue into the game, skating it along her pounding clit, heat filled her veins. A climax rumbled through her like an earthquake, starting deep in her core and welling upward. Whatever point Ava had been trying to make, Charlie got it loud and clear. As she came down from a fuzzy post-orgasmic cloud, Charlie vowed to put a sock in her tiresome displays of jealousy.

CHAPTER SEVENTEEN

"How many times have you FaceTimed?" Liz asked.

"Hm, only every day since she left," Charlie replied.

"Jesus, Charlie. Give the woman a break. You're smothering her from fifteen hundred miles away."

"I'm doing my best, Liz." Charlie suppressed a sigh. She'd wanted to dash home after the last scene of the day and chat with Ava online, but Liz had demanded they go for a drink.

"That may very well be. I'm just giving you some friendly advice, that's all." Liz sipped from her beer.

"Sometimes..." Perhaps Liz had the right idea. Since Charlie had waved off Ava's car last Saturday, she'd felt like she'd been holding onto something invisible and unnamable. Like she'd been dancing on a tightrope and if she slipped off, something inside her would come loose. Seeing Ava's face on her laptop screen on a daily basis seemed to be the only cure for the insecurities lodged inside her mind. "I feel like I don't know how it works anymore. How to behave and carry myself in this new relationship. I have all this baggage and, excuse the poor metaphor, it's weighing heavy on me."

"You're overcompensating because you're apart. It's normal. But it may result in you not giving your young affair enough breathing room to blossom."

"It doesn't help that I have a paparazzi parked outside my house these days." Charlie stared at her half-empty glass of beer. Ava being away for a few weeks wasn't so much the problem. Charlie had, at the very least, functioned properly before Ava had entered her life. She went to bed on time, obeyed the early morning chime of her alarm clock, ate decent enough food, and spent time on the treadmill. Now, because Ava had occupied a space in her life that she'd been so desperate to fill, her absence felt unbearable. Charlie drank the better part of a bottle of wine every evening, the curtains drawn—lest a photographer snapped a candid shot of her gorging on Pinot Gris.

"You're welcome to stay at ours if it would help," Liz offered.

"I need to stop feeling sorry for myself. If only I knew how."

Liz regarded her with a funny look on her face.

"What?" Charlie asked.

"The answer is so simple you might want to punch me in the face when I tell you." She accompanied her statement with a grin.

"Then please don't keep me in suspense any longer."

"Just live, Charlie. Live your awesome life." Liz held her hands in front of her face and ducked behind them.

"You're lucky I'm not a violent person, Lizzie. You're safe."

"I know you were an emotional mess when you came to LA, but so many great things have happened to you since then."

"Yeah, like my ex moving here." Charlie pushed her beer away. She needed to drink water instead. "For the record, I'm only joking. I'm good with it, as long as she stays away from me."

"That's the thing with you, Charlie. You always have a condition. Things are great with Ava, as long as you're in the same city. You're over Jo, as long as you're *not* in the same city. Do you recognize a pattern here?"

"What are you saying?" Charlie started fiddling with her beer glass again. "That I should become friends with my ex?"

"Not necessarily. Just that it's not always someone or something else's fault."

Charlie's hackles went up. She grabbed the glass and drank the remainder in three large gulps. "I know I have many faults, Liz."

"We all do." Liz shrugged. "So what?" Liz eyed Charlie's empty glass. "I want this to work out for you. I know how strongly you feel about Ava. Just give it a decent chance. I do think you're ready, but just... I don't know, take things slowly, let them develop at a natural pace and... don't give her too hard a time about being enough of a lesbian."

"I'm doing my best. I really am. But I'm afraid my best won't be enough."

"Trust me, buddy. Your best is usually more than enough."

Charlie met Liz's gaze. "Do you think I should see Jo? She's going to be here for another few months. I'm surprised I haven't run into her yet, to be honest."

Liz nodded thoughtfully, but didn't respond.

Charlie continued, "It's just that, in my head, she's grown into this monster. This woman who deserted me for no good reason—for a man. In truth, we shared a number of happy years together."

"Why not? What have you got to lose by seeing her?"

Only my mind. Charlie was over-dramatizing again. "I think I will. Before Ava comes back. It might help me put some things into perspective."

"Good." Liz nodded like a satisfied school teacher. "Now, for the elephant in the room."

"I knew you were stalling by giving me a speech, Lizzie." Charlie was, of course, playing dumb. Liz was, of course, referring to her lackluster commitment to the softball team.

"I fully understand you've been too preoccupied for softball practice, and I also understand you were hiding under too thick a blanket of self-pity on Sunday to come to the game. In fact, we both know this isn't about softball. But you need to say something to Josie. How do you think she felt when she saw the person who won the date with her all over Facebook, hand-in-hand with Ava Castaneda?"

"I know." Charlie shook her head. "I'll call her."

Liz cocked her head.

"Soon. Tonight, after we go home. I promise."

"You'd better."

"What are the rules for this sort of situation?" Charlie asked in earnest. "Does the date have to be consummated?"

Liz visibly tensed. "It's just a date, Charlie. A date can be grabbing a cup of coffee at Starbucks. It doesn't have to be a spectacle. The main goal of the auction was to raise money, and we've far exceeded all our expectations on that front. But I certainly wouldn't want anyone's feelings to get hurt because of it."

"Understood." She fell back into her chair. "Sometimes I wish I could fast-forward a few years. Of course, on the condition that Ava and I stay together, and just be done with all these doubts and nerves that come with the very beginning of a relationship."

"Don't say that. Every stage of a relationship has its place and virtue." A smile came over Liz's face. "I remember courting Sarah. While it's true I was a nervous, mumbling wreck for the better part of it, I have nothing but fond memories."

"Perhaps, but so much can go wrong as well."

Liz slanted her head and looked at her in silence for a few long seconds.

"What?" Charlie asked.

"Well, you haven't been very detailed in your descriptions, but I do take it you and Ava have... you know..."

Charlie chuckled. "Fucked?"

"Fucked?" Liz's mouth fall open and she covered it with her hands. "You mean two women can *fuck*? Even the notion!"

"I know. How would they do it, right? It's anatomically impossible. Where do we get the right to even call it that? I really don't know." Charlie enjoyed the chuckle that rippled through her.

"Okay. Enough of that." Liz playfully slapped the table with the palm of her hand, a wide smile on her face. "Indulge me, Charlie. What's it like to have sex with Ava Castaneda?"

"You're not wearing a wire, are you?" Charlie jokingly looked around for people listening.

"Oh, please." Liz pulled her lips into an offended pout.

"I'm not of any religious affiliation, but I believe one could compare it to going to heaven," Charlie said solemnly. "Also, I as good as came in my pants the very first time, but I digress."

"You didn't?" Liz slapped the table again. "How is that even possible?"

"Remain untouched for long enough and... boom!" Charlie mimicked an explosion of fireworks with her fingers.

"So, you and Ava were kissing, and you came in your pants. Then what happened?"

"Oh, screw you. I knew I shouldn't have told anyone about this, least of all you. I'm never going to live it down, am I?"

"Come on, Charlie. Remember how to take a joke?"

"This stays between you and me, okay? You don't

even tell Sarah!"

"But we're lesbians," Liz said. "We tell each other everything. How will our relationship survive?"

"Stop it. I think you've had enough, by the way, Lizzie. Why don't I walk you home?"

"I'm just messing with you." Liz relaxed in her chair. "Let's have another."

CHAPTER EIGHTEEN

Knives Out shot every season in a different American city. When Charlie landed in Dallas, she hoped that the next season would be filmed in San Diego or, even better, Santa Barbara. The flight was only two-and-a-half hours, but Charlie didn't have the sort of job where she could close her office door at five. She wasn't the showrunner for *Underground*. Still, it felt like her show. Her brain had birthed the characters and, together with Liz and the other writers, she had crafted the lines of dialogue the actors spoke in front of the camera when they embodied her characters.

To her surprise, Charlie found it difficult to leave LA and not be there for an early Saturday morning shoot. Her presence wasn't required, but it felt a little like leaving behind a child for the very first time.

By the time she boarded the plane, Charlie was so tired, she fell into an uncomfortable slumber. Despite being exhausted from a long week with early mornings and late nights on set, Charlie's brain refused to relax enough to allow her to drift off peacefully.

She hadn't seen Ava in two weeks. She would arrive at Ava's hotel in the middle of the night, and Ava was scheduled for an early wake-up call the next morning. If she wanted, Charlie could join her on set, but they would only truly be together later that day and in between shots. Charlie had to leave Dallas on Sunday evening and had to be on set at six in the morning on Monday for one of the biggest *Underground* scenes of the season. It was the type of scene that defined a show and gave the star, Elisa Fox, a chance to show them that she was worth the astronomical fee the network was paying her. Charlie wasn't going to miss that, even though she'd probably only be allowed to watch from a small screen in someone's trailer because Elisa had demanded a closed set.

Charlie could have opted to stay in LA of course. No one would have minded. But she had to see Ava. The real reason was easy enough to disguise in this lovey-dovey stage they were still in. She had to see Ava, and she had to see Eric and Ava together. She had to see for herself how they acted around each other.

Charlie lay with a face mask pulled tightly over her eyes, her neck sore from being forced into an uncomfortable position, and went over her reasons again. She felt terribly small-minded, petty, and jealous. But she was convinced that if she could just reassure herself, everything would be all right from then on. For Charlie, it was an important step.

After spending an hour in self-enforced darkness with noise-canceling headphones covering her ears, Charlie had had enough. The cabin lights were dimmed when she took off her mask and, as though she had been waiting for her to wake up, a flight attendant was by her side within seconds.

"May I get you a beverage, Miss Cross?" she asked.

From her tone, Charlie could glean this particular flight attendant was up to speed on all things Hollywood gossip—and probably even knew why Charlie was flying to Dallas.

"White wine, please."

"Right away." She sped off, only to return within minutes with an empty glass and a bottle of Pinot Gris. She lowered the built-in tray, set the glass on it, and presented the label of the wine to Charlie before pouring.

As she filled Charlie's glass, she smiled so broadly, Charlie feared her cheeks might stay cramped in that position forever.

"Keep it coming, please," Charlie said, shooting the flight attendant a practiced smile in return.

Charlie drank, and the familiar sensation of a chilled drink hitting her palate calmed her nerves. She checked her watch and counted the hours until she would see Ava.

* * *

A car sent by the *Knives Out* production team picked Charlie up from the airport. It was past midnight and traffic was easy. Charlie made it to Ava's hotel by one in the morning, and an extra key was waiting for her at reception.

Charlie knocked very quietly before inserting the card into the electronic lock. Her heart banged inexplicably against her ribs. It wasn't like she thought she'd find Eric in bed with Ava. The room was silent, and Charlie let herself in as quietly as she could.

"Ava?" she whispered. A dim nightlight by the door didn't help Charlie to see very well and the room was so eerily quiet, Charlie thought it might be empty. While her eyes adjusted to the darkness—she didn't want to turn on the light and wake Ava—she made her way farther into the room. The sheets on the bed were folded back as if someone had just gotten up.

Charlie started to wonder if she had the right room, when someone grabbed her from behind.

"Charlie Cross," Ava whispered in her ear, "I'm so delighted you came." She folded her long arms around Charlie's waist.

"Jesus fucking Christ!" Charlie screamed. "I nearly

jumped out of my skin."

"Why don't you start by jumping out of your clothes instead?" Ava spun Charlie around in her embrace. "I missed you."

"Fuck." Charlie was still recovering from Ava's prank. "Don't ever do that again. I think you shaved a few years off my life."

"Did you really think I would be sleeping when you arrived?" Ava's eyes sparkled in the low light. "I wouldn't let you come all this way for that, baby."

"Don't you have a wake-up call at six or some other ungodly hour?" Charlie melted under Ava's gaze.

Ava nodded. "I believe that gives us five hours." Ava brought her face within inches of Charlie's. "Did you bring that present you promised?"

Instantly, Charlie flushed with heat. She'd ordered it on the internet and then picked up the package from the post office herself because there was no one home when the mailman rang her bell—it wasn't the sort of package she would send an assistant to get for her. It had been one of the more stressful moments of her life, but it had been discreetly wrapped and the nondescript box could have held anything.

"I did." Charlie smiled.

"Let's save that for tomorrow though. Tonight, I want to feel you." Ava pushed Charlie toward the bed. "I want to fuck you, Charlie. So badly."

"That's what I'm here for," Charlie joked. A knot uncoiled in her stomach, and she felt foolish for having worried.

Ava meant business and, in one quick movement, pulled the tank top she was wearing over her head. Charlie swallowed hard at the sight of Ava partially naked and reaching for her.

"Let's get these clothes off you." Ava's hands were all over Charlie in an instant. "Do you want to take a shower?"

Charlie nodded, and Ava disposed of all of their clothes in no time. "How about you kiss me first?" Charlie asked. And only then, when they were both completely naked, did Ava press her lips to Charlie's.

Lust and pure happiness rushed through Charlie. Liz had been right. Fast-forwarding to a time when this feeling would become less intense would be against all rules of relationships—and humanity. Charlie returned Ava's kiss, pulled her close, and let her hands roam the expanse of Ava's soft, soft skin.

When they broke from their kiss, Ava said, "Let me show you how grateful I am to you for coming all this way." She held out her hand. "Come on."

The bathroom boasted a huge walk-in shower, and Ava pushed Charlie inside.

"Still bossy then," Charlie said.

"Don't pretend you don't like it." Ava stood there with a huge smirk on her face, and her hand on the faucet. "Let's get you nicely soaped up." She flipped the tab up and water rained down on them. The first few seconds it was cold, and Charlie's nipples hardened to even stiffer knots. Ava grabbed a tube of shower gel from the alcove in the wall and squirted a considerable amount into her palm. "Hands up, Charlie."

Charlie could hardly pretend she hadn't come here to comply with Ava's wishes. And this time, not only would it be logistically impossible for her to come in her pants—Ava had tugged them off her already—but she *had* taken matters into her own hands during Ava's absence.

Ava lathered her with soap. She began with Charlie's belly.

"You're tickling me," Charlie complained.

"Too soft a touch for you, huh? I'll remember that." Mischief shined in Ava's eyes. She worked her way up to

Charlie's breasts and kneaded them ever so softly, her caresses aided by the foam. Charlie's clit pulsed between her legs like a second heart. She might not be coming in her pants, but she was well on her way to a hands-free orgasm if Ava kept this up.

Charlie leaned against the glass wall, panting, hands above her head. Some of the foam transferred to Ava's body and the bright white color of the bubbly soap against Ava's caramel skin made Charlie's mouth water.

Meanwhile, Ava washed—though that was too generous a description for it—Charlie by letting her hands drift across her skin the way they did when they made love.

"Keep your hands up," Ava said. "Spread your legs."

"Yes, ma'am," Charlie joked.

Ava stopped abruptly. "Am I *too* bossy? I have no desire to be called ma'am." Her face was serious.

"I was just kidding." Charlie shot Ava a quick wink.

"I guess we'll have to talk about this at some point, but not now." Ava went back to work, and her hands migrated to Charlie's ass. "Turn around," she said.

Charlie spun around and kept her legs spread. She was glad for the respite of being able to look away from Ava for a few minutes, despite traveling all this way to lay eyes on her. She was dizzy with lust, her clit buzzing, her nipples aching so much they hurt. For the briefest of instants, while she stood facing the glass wall, Charlie tried to remember if it had ever been like this with Jo. But then Ava started distributing soap on her ass cheeks with a touch so soft and subtle, Charlie wasn't sure the moisture seeping between her legs came from the shower or straight from the wetness of her pussy.

"Let's get you nice and clean, Charlie," Ava said, her voice hoarse. Ava's fingers skidded along Charlie's skin, setting her on fire, despite the water raining down on them.

Ava's hands had reached Charlie's inner thighs, and Charlie sucked in a deep breath as Ava slipped her fingers along Charlie's wet folds. "Oh, Christ," she muttered.

"Don't come like this," Ava whispered in her ear as she contoured her body to Charlie's. Her fingers worked inside Charlie as Ava said, "I want to see you."

Charlie didn't know how she was supposed to follow that command. Especially now that Ava's fingertips brushed her clit as they moved slinkily between her legs.

"Turn around," Ava whispered finally.

By the time Charlie stood with her back against the wall, her breath came in sharp gusts, and all she wanted was for Ava to kiss her and plunge her soap-lubed fingers deep inside of her.

"Tell me what you want, Charlie?" Ava asked instead. As if she didn't know. Charlie was beginning to suspect Ava got a perverse pleasure out of teasing her to the extreme.

"Jesus, will you just fuck me?" Charlie spread her legs wide in invitation.

Ava tipped her head to the side. With one hand pressed against the glass wall next to Charlie's head, the other was free to do whatever Charlie wanted—or what Ava chose to do with it. "Say it again." Ava tickled Charlie's tortured pussy lips.

Or maybe it turned Ava on to hear Charlie say it out loud like that. "Fuck me," Charlie said, testing.

Ava brought her face closer to Charlie's. "With how many fingers?" Ava was clearly close to unraveling.

"Th-three." Charlie breathed heavily.

Ava brought three fingers to Charlie's face. They were slick with soap and water. Ava dragged them down her cheek, then all the way down her chest—passing between her breasts—until she reached Charlie's sex.

"As you wish." Ava stared into her eyes and entered Charlie.

"Ooh," Charlie moaned. She would fly across the globe for this moment. For this split second when Ava claimed her. For that first instant of complete intimate reconnection when all thoughts fled Charlie's brain and everything was right in her world.

"Fuck, I'm crazy about you, Charlie." Ava stared into her eyes. She delved deep inside Charlie's pussy, stealing her breath and her last rational thought. "I don't know what you've done to me." Ava thrust just that much faster, and Charlie started to fall apart. More because of Ava's words than the increased pace. Ava was crazy about her? Everything smelled like soap and her field of vision narrowed until all she could see was Ava. Charlie ached as though someone had lit a fire in her belly, and her orgasm swept through her in one big gulf of pleasure, seizing all her muscles.

"Oh fuck," Charlie groaned. "I'm crazy about you too." She dropped her head onto Ava's shoulders and showered her in kisses. Ava's fingers were still inside of her, and although they had done their job expertly, Charlie wanted them to remain inside of her forever— she wanted a piece of Ava with her for when they had to part again.

Then Ava eased her fingers out of Charlie's pussy with soft tenderness.

"I think you might be dirty again," she said. "I may need to wash you all over again."

They both burst out in a silly bout of laughter, and Charlie was sure that what she'd said in the throes of passion was the absolute truth.

CHAPTER NINETEEN

The telephone rang at six in the morning and was a rude awakening for both of them. But all it took for Charlie was one quick glimpse at Ava, and her mood turned from sleep-deprived cranky to utterly blissful.

"Do you want to come? I can send a car for you later? Either way, it might be boring for you. Loads of waiting."

"I can think of something to make the waiting go by faster." Charlie sat up and fixed her gaze on the box she'd brought all the way from LA.

Ava grinned, but shook her head. "No, Charlie. Not when I'm working. Makeup will have a fit if I come back from my trailer with a just-fucked look."

"Okay. I wouldn't want you to be worried about your hair the first time we fuck like that."

"Thank you for respecting my means of employment." Ava draped an arm over Charlie's belly.

"Ready for your shower?" Charlie dug her fingertips into Ava's arm.

"Stop, before you make me too horny again." Ava swatted Charlie's hand away. "I really have to get going. Wash your pussy scent off me." Ava giggled, and Charlie giggled with her.

Ava slipped from the bed and walked into the bathroom totally naked. She was barely awake, but a fresh round of thumping had already ignited in Charlie's clit. She felt it in her stomach, too, as an endless dance of butterflies. Content, Charlie sagged back into the pillows. She was tempted to close her eyes again and catch up on some much-needed sleep, but she'd come here to spend time with Ava, so that was what she would do.

* * *

Ava had been right. The set of *Knives Out* quickly became a snooze fest for Charlie, what with the many retakes and countless times Ava's makeup was being reapplied.

Charlie decided there wasn't much glamour to be found in reality television. Eric wasn't due on set that morning, something Charlie first viewed as lucky, but then, as her boredom grew, it annoyed her. It made her think too much about the other reason why she had flown to Dallas. Yes, she wanted to spend time with Ava, but she also wanted to see Ava interact with Eric. That was hard to do when he wasn't around.

"You should go back to the hotel," Ava said during a break. "Get some sleep. I'll meet you there as soon as I can."

Charlie looked around. If she hadn't just spent the past few weeks on the set of *Underground*, perhaps staying would have held some appeal. As it was, seeing Ava repeat the same lines of text over and over again was fun the first ten minutes, but the novelty quickly wore off. Charlie also suspected she might be throwing Ava off her game somewhat. When she was introducing a cooking challenge to the contestants earlier, the director had sighed with exasperation, and Ava had sent him an apologetic smirk.

"I think I just might." Charlie looked at Ava. Up close, only her eyes looked tired—the makeup people had done an expert job at hiding any other remnants of the near sleepless night they'd just had. "I'll let you sleep tonight, I promise." She smiled encouragingly at Ava.

"We'll see about that."

* * *

On the way back to the hotel, Charlie concluded that, from this set visit, she'd gained a newfound respect for reality television show hosts. The car pulled up to the entrance of the hotel and Charlie's legs felt weary when she got out.

"Charlie Cross," a male voice said as Charlie entered the lobby. A male voice that made her cringe. Charlie turned around and looked into Eric's wrinkled face. If only Ava could have traded schedules with him—but she was the host and her presence on the *Knives Out* set was much more required than the head judge's.

"Eric." Charlie tried a polite nod of the head.

"I believe I owe you an apology," he said. "Can I buy you a drink?"

Charlie sighed inwardly. She just wanted to go to sleep. She didn't want to spend time with Eric, but she sympathized with him on some level, and he did say the word "apology." It would be rude to refuse. "Sure." She tried to inject some lightness into her tone.

"Awesome. I know just the place." He flashed a smile. "By that, I mean the hotel bar isn't horrible."

They walked to the elevator bank and Eric pushed the button for the top floor. Once they were seated at the bar, Charlie ordered a margarita and, upon hearing her order, Eric asked for the same.

"Screw those who think a margarita is a girlie drink. It's no such thing. Right, Charlie?"

"Right." Charlie wondered when he would launch into that apology.

Eric turned on his stool to face her better, and the two of them sitting at the bar like that reminded Charlie of the last time she'd seen him. Eric fixed her with a strange stare. His eyes were watery, and his skin was a bit puffy. "I know I acted like a grade-A asshole that Sunday. Will you accept my apology?"

Which apology? Just then, the barkeep deposited two huge margaritas—certainly too large for the middle of the afternoon—in front of them.

"Ah, right in time for a toast," Eric said. He picked up his glass and held it out to Charlie.

Charlie was nowhere near ready to forgive him, but she clinked her cocktail glass against his anyway.

"I'm an all right dude, Charlie," he said after touching his glass to hers briefly.

"I'm sure you are," Charlie replied. *Otherwise you wouldn't be Ava's friend*, she added in her head. She sipped her drink and the alcohol tasted much stronger than she expected. Or perhaps it was the lack of sleep and food— Charlie had only eaten a muffin for breakfast and a bagel for lunch on the *Knives Out* set. "Whoa. They sure know how to pack a punch in their margaritas."

"Told you I knew a good place. When we're on location a good bar is crucial. And by good, I mean generous with the alcohol." Eric sighed loudly. "Aah, that's nice."

"You're not shooting today?" Charlie asked, frustrated that she had to sit here in Eric's company instead of Ava's.

"Nope. My services are not required today. I took the opportunity to have lunch with Armand Van Cleef at his restaurant. It was absolutely delicious. Chicken liver casserole."

Charlie's stomach turned. Chicken liver casserole sounded far from delicious to her, but what did she know? She wasn't a chef. She took another sip from her margarita to settle it. It wasn't the best idea, but it was all she had.

"Ava cooks a mean chicken liver. Has she prepared

it for you yet?" Eric rested his watery gaze on her.

"God no. And I'd prefer if she never did, either," Charlie replied, not meeting his eyes.

"You don't know what you're missing." Eric made quick work of his margarita. According to Nick's rules of fashion for men, Eric wore his shirt with one too many buttons open. A tuft of grey chest hair peeked out at the top.

Charlie wasn't accustomed to making middle-aged straight men open up to her. With Nick, all she needed was one word and he'd spill his innermost secrets, but this rather gruff man next to her—who had clearly started drinking before they sat down together for margaritas—was still an enigma to her. And she desperately wanted to know more.

"Another?" she asked, pointing at Eric's near-empty glass.

"Don't mind if I do." He signaled the bartender and, without consulting Charlie, ordered two more.

They made some small talk about *Knives Out* and *Underground*, and Eric told Charlie about his very first job as a dishwasher in New York. By the time Charlie finished her second margarita, Eric was halfway through his fourth.

"I almost convinced her to move to New York with me, you know?" he said out of the blue. "Only the most magnificent city in the world."

During her time in LA, Charlie had missed New York terribly, but she was more focused on the first part of Eric's statement.

"But she's a Los Angeles woman through and through."

Charlie assumed he was talking about Ava.

"Some women… they leave a lasting impact, you know?" he continued to muse. "You like women, Charlie. You should know." He regarded her, and his eyes seemed to be sunk even deeper into their sockets.

Despite being unsettled by what Eric said, Charlie took the opportunity to pry with both hands. "You sound as though you may still have some lingering feelings for Ava."

Eric uttered a weird half chuckle. "Lingering," he said, then shook his head. He took a few more sips. Charlie did the same. She needed the liquid courage for the rest of this conversation. Despite not knowing Eric, a half-drunk man was more likely to tell her the truth than a man with his guard up.

"What happened the other—" Charlie started to say, but Eric cut her off.

"No offense, Charlie. I'm sure you're a fine girl and all that, but you and Ava…" He hung his head and shook it. "No. Just no. I can see why she's with you. Strangely enough, I really can. You're young and fresh and something completely different, but she's a fickle woman. I should know."

Blind panic shot through Charlie. What Eric was saying didn't make the most sense, but it did feed Charlie's ever-present paranoia.

"I know she had that… thing with Sandra, but Ava is no lesbian. I can attest to that. Pardon my French, Charlie, but she won't go long without cock." He had the audacity to stare her straight in the eyes. "My advice to you—get out while you can. Now. While it won't hurt too much." He narrowed his eyes a bit. "Three-and-a-half weeks may not seem long in the grand scheme of things, but these location shoots can feel like they go on forever and—I'm about to tell you a secret here, Charlie—not a season has gone by, and we shoot two per year, when Ava hasn't done some really raunchy things with my cock." He grinned without baring his teeth, almost apologetically. "What can I say? I know what she likes."

Charlie's stomach churned, her insides roiling and

threatening to climb up her esophagus. Instantly, an image of Ava in bed with Eric lodged itself in her mind. Right next to the barely faded one of Jo and Christian. That particular picture wouldn't disappear from her brain any time soon.

"You're drunk. And you're full of shit," Charlie managed to say.

He pulled his grey eyebrows into arcs on his forehead. "Am I?" He sucked his lips into his mouth to add extra confusion to his last question. "I've known her for ten years, Charlie. How long have you known her?"

He's just playing you to get her back, Charlie repeated to herself in her head. "I know what you're trying to do here. Apologize my ass." Charlie slid off her stool. "It's not going to work, you jealous, homophobic prick."

She didn't cast him a further glance and sped out of the bar. When she reached the elevator, though, Charlie's heart was pounding so fast she had to steady herself against the wall. On the way down to Ava's room, her stomach twisted itself in a dozen more knots and, as soon as Charlie reached the room, she fled into the bathroom and hurled out the remnants of the margaritas.

She sat gasping for air over the toilet, her cheeks tear-stained, her body cramped. Despite a persistent voice in her head telling her that leaving would only give Eric what he wanted, Charlie couldn't do this. She couldn't return to LA and live with the image he'd put in her head. Charlie had gone through it once before—the endless comparing herself to a man. That never-ending useless, painful train of thought that asked *If she wasn't good enough for Jo, then how could she ever be for Ava?*

The dark months after her breakup with Jo suddenly came back to her with humiliating clarity. Anything—even life without Ava—was better than that.

Charlie didn't have a lot to pack. Once she'd picked up the clothes Ava had stripped off her the night before, she went online and changed her flight home.

Whether she'd say goodbye to Ava before fleeing depended on Ava's shooting schedule. Charlie had two hours before she needed to leave for the airport.

CHAPTER TWENTY

"Charl-ie," Ava sang out brightly when she entered the room. "I convinced them to let me go earlier than planned today. Some days, right?" She mock-sighed.

Charlie had been sitting in the same spot on the bed for an hour, not moving an inch, alternately cursing and convincing herself that she was making the right decision—maybe not in anyone else's eyes, but for herself.

"Charlie?" Ava dropped her purse. "I thought you'd be in bed. Fully strapped-on. Are you all right?"

A bolt of fear rushed through Charlie, nestling somewhere in her stomach. "I can't do this, Ava. I'm very sorry, but I can't."

"Can't do what?" Ava crouched in front of her, resting her hands on Charlie's knees. "Strap it on?" She looked at Charlie's packed carry-on case. "Are you going somewhere?" The glee in her voice was quickly being replaced by something less cheerful.

"I had a chat with Eric. I'm sure half of what he told me isn't true, but he got under my skin, and that's the real problem here."

"Eric? What did he say?" Ava's fingernails dug into Charlie's jeans.

"Just… some things I really didn't want to hear." The image invaded Charlie's brain again.

"That bastard." Ava pushed herself up and started pacing. "Don't listen to him, Charlie. Whatever he has said, it's nothing but a pathetic display of jealousy."

"I thought he was your friend?" Charlie said. "He clearly thinks he's much more than that."

Ava stopped pacing, scanned the room briefly, then sat down next to Charlie. "For some reason, Eric has it in his head that he and I are meant to be together. Maybe it's his midlife crisis. I don't know. Either way, I made it clear to him that I don't feel the same way."

"But you did sleep with him."

Ava expelled a deep sigh. "Yes. Once. When you and I weren't talking. You know that. Nothing else has happened." Irritation colored the edges of Ava's tone. "What am I defending myself against here? You know how I feel about you."

"What about before we met? All those lonely nights away from home on location."

"What? What about them, Charlie?" Ava stood again.

"You told me you and he broke up five years ago and you'd both moved on since then. You never said that you were 'friends with benefits.'"

"We are no such thing." Ava leaned against the wall facing Charlie. "This is getting ridiculous."

"So you never slept with him on location?"

"For Christ's sake. Is this an investigation into my honor and virtue?" Ava closed her eyes. "I'm tired as hell, Charlie. I can't have this conversation. Not now. And not ever, for that matter."

"We don't need to." Charlie rose from the bed. "I changed my flight. I'm going home."

"Charlie." It was more a sigh than a word coming from Ava's mouth. "You're giving him exactly what he wants. Don't you see that?"

"I do." Every muscle in Charlie's body tightened. She had no idea how she would make it to the door. "I'm the problem here. I know that. I wish I could help it.

But… I just can't."

"What about me?" Ava had taken a few steps in Charlie's direction. "Don't I mean more to you than all these crazy thoughts in your head?"

A tear leaked from Charlie's eye. "You do, but Eric was right about one thing." She swallowed hard before she continued. "It's better for me to leave now, before it hurts even more."

Ava's facial expression changed from tender anguish to frustrated anger. "If you leave now, this is over. I did my part, said my piece. I won't be coming after you again, Charlie. I don't need all your bullshit, anyway. Go home and grow the fuck up." She wiped a tear from her cheek. "If you prefer to trust Eric's words over mine, then you're right, you'd better leave now."

Charlie just nodded, turned on her heels, and headed for the door. It fell into the lock behind her with the softest of thuds.

* * *

Charlie arrived in LA in the middle of the night. While she waited for a taxi, she tried to decide between what seemed like her two best choices. Option one—go home, take an Ambien, sleep it off, and try to pick up her life again in the morning. Option two—tell the driver to drop her at Nick and Jason's house where she could cry for a few more hours before taking an Ambien, sleeping it off, and trying to pick up her life the next morning.

Nick would show her no mercy. He would tell her exactly what the faults in her logic were. It was precisely that sort of chastising Charlie was after. She needed someone to tell her how she had failed, to unclog the cobwebs from her mind, to free her from the illusion that every woman was always going to hurt her the same way Jo had.

By the time she got into the backseat of a taxi, Charlie was convinced she didn't deserve the relief of a sedative or the all-forgiving embrace of easy sleep without first being called on her crap. She needed to be told off. She directed the driver to Nick and Jason's house. When she stood in front of their door, she checked her watch. It was two in the morning. Nick wouldn't be happy about being woken from his beauty sleep, but Jason would want her to come by when she was this distressed.

Then there was the faintest hint of a drum beat, followed by a shriek of laughter. Were they still up? It was Saturday, after all. She hesitated. What kind of person barged in on friends while they were entertaining? And God knew who was at their house.

Charlie checked her watch again. Rude or not, she didn't want to go home. With a heavy heart, she rang the bell.

Voices rose from the back of the house, and she heard the telltale sound of footfalls as someone approached. It sounded like high heels coming toward the door, and Charlie half-expected Nick to appear dressed in drag. An anticipatory smile started to form on her lips.

The door swung open and Charlie's smile faded.

"Charlie!" Jo said.

"Oh, God," was all Charlie could utter.

"Charlie, come in!" Jo was clearly drunk. "What time is it? You're rather late to the party." Jo pulled at Charlie's arm, then noticed her suitcase. "Are you going somewhere?"

"What is going on here?" Nick, in jeans and wrinkled shirt, came to the door. "Charlie?" He squinted while looking from Charlie to Jo, and then back to Charlie. "I won't ask what you're doing here. Just come in, will you?"

Charlie stepped inside the house, which was now the last place she wanted to be. Jo was tipsy, but she still looked scrumptious in those tight jeans and that boat-neck top that bared her shoulder.

"Why aren't you in Dallas?" Nick said, as he led Charlie into the living room. Jason walked toward her and kissed her on the cheeks, but then—as if she still hadn't sunk low enough that day—she noticed Christian sitting at the head of the table.

"I've been wondering where you've been hiding, Charlie," Jo said jovially, as though they were old acquaintances and not ex-lovers.

Christian rose from his chair and approached Charlie, hand extended. "Charlie," he said.

Charlie looked at his hand as if it was a grenade someone had just pulled the pin out of. As far as worst nights of her life went, this one was quickly climbing the ranks, with the night after Jo had finally told her she was in love with Christian still firmly in the lead.

Nick nudged her in the elbow and, still dazed, Charlie shook Christian's hand.

"This is a surprise," Jason said. "Please, sit, Charlie. We've all had a bit too much, so excuse any raunchiness."

The sight of the four of them together, in the midst of an obviously joyous evening in each other's company hit Charlie square in the chest. Jason using the word raunchiness, as Eric had earlier in reference to Ava, combined with unexpectedly seeing Jo and Christian together, crashed together in Charlie's brain, to create a void of static and white noise. As if observing herself from a distance, she first noticed the way her legs failed her, followed by her core muscles refusing to hold her upright as her body crumpled in on itself, all while tears streamed down her cheeks.

What sort of a mind-fuck was this, anyway? Would Eric be jumping out of a closet soon, point his finger at her and say, "Ha, ha. Gotcha!"

"Charlie!" Nick rushed to her side and threw his arms around her. "Hey, come on. I've got you." He guided her toward the guestroom down the hall and set her down on the bed. "It's okay, Jase. I've got this." Through her tears, Charlie made out Jason's lanky figure standing by the door.

"Charlie, honey. What happened to you?" Nick tilted Charlie's head toward his shoulder and patted her hair.

But Charlie couldn't speak. The body parts responsible for speech weren't working. Noises came from the living room. All Charlie could do was cry on Nick's shoulder, loud, heaving sobs filled with self-pity.

"We'll talk tomorrow, honey." Nick's voice was too sweet. It didn't match his public image. Beneath his cultivated cynicism, he was all kindness and concern for his friends. "You sleep here. Annie will keep you company. She'll love it. You know how crazy she is about you."

Rather than leave, Nick sat with Charlie for what felt like hours. Apart from the careful clattering of dishes and the patter of excited paws in the hallway, the rest of the house was quiet. Jo and Christian must have left.

"Do you want me to undress you?" Nick asked. This helped snap Charlie out of her morose state a bit.

"What would the world have come to if I wanted that," she said, but there was no laughter in her voice.

"I'll get your suitcase and some water, okay?"

Charlie nodded. "Do you have any sleeping pills?"

"Of course." Nick opened the door a slit, and Annie ran into the room, yelping enthusiastically.

"Come on, you silly dog," Charlie said, and patted the spot next to her on the bed. "Hop on."

The dog kept on leaping up and down on her tiny legs; the bed was too high for her. She picked her up.

"Hey you, with all your unconditional love. You could surely teach me a thing or two." Charlie buried her nose in Annie's soft fur.

A knock on the door announced Nick's arrival. He put a bottle of water on the nightstand and two pills next to it. He walked over to pet Annie and, wholly against Charlie's expectations, plant a kiss on the top of Charlie's head.

"We'll talk tomorrow. Sleep tight," he said and gave Charlie's shoulder one last squeeze before exiting the room, leaving the door ajar.

CHAPTER TWENTY-ONE

"Good morning, gorgeous." Jason looked up from his iPad.

"Let's be honest here, Jase. She's looked better." Nick rose from his chair on the terrace where they were having a late breakfast. "Did you manage to get some sleep?" He pulled a chair out for Charlie, as if she were visiting a fancy restaurant. Next, he'd be putting a napkin in her lap.

"The sleep of the drugged," Charlie said.

"We're having some hair of the dog. No offense, my darling Annie." He reached for Annie, who was still by Charlie's side when she woke up, and deposited the dog in his lap. "Would you like a mimosa?"

"Sure. Why not?" Charlie took the seat Nick had offered her. "Guys, I'm so sorry about last night. I couldn't face going to my empty house, but, of course, I wouldn't have come if I had known…"

Jason poured her half a glass of champagne, then topped it off with freshly squeezed orange juice.

"What happened?" Finally, the first hint of impatience in Nick's voice. This didn't irritate Charlie so much as make her feel at home.

Charlie inhaled deeply, then sipped her mimosa. It hit her bloodstream hard, considering she hadn't eaten anything since leaving Dallas. "I got into an, erm, argument with Ava. We broke up. It's over. It's my fault."

"Jesus, Charlie. For a woman who can write page

upon page of the craziest lesbian drama, you're being very sparse with your words today," Nick said.

Jason and Nick exchanged a glance.

"Take your time, Charlie," Jason, an angel Nick had somehow lured from heaven, said. "We have all day. Nick and I are here for you. You know that."

This almost made her well up again. Annie leaped off Jason's lap and yelped at Charlie's toes.

Charlie did her best to explain about her encounter with Eric and the seeds of doubt he'd planted in her mind.

"You just left her there? In the room?" Nick asked.

"I know." Even though Charlie was fully aware that what she had done was inexcusable and very hurtful, she couldn't think of any conceivable way she could have stopped herself from doing it.

"You do know that Eric was lying, right?" Nick's gaze on her intensified. He was getting ready to crucify her.

Charlie stopped herself from asking if Nick knew about Eric and Ava hooking up while on location because it would set Nick off even more. And it didn't matter anymore. "Charlie, Charlie, Charlie." Instead of scolding further, he just sat there, shaking his head. "You're my friend, but so is Ava, and so is Jo. When are you going to stop hurting my friends?"

Charlie leaned back a bit in her chair. "Me hurt them? That's not how all this started, Nickie."

Nick puffed out some air through his nose. "I've had enough of this, Charlie." He steepled his fingers together. "I also have a plan." He stood. "Jase, don't let her leave. Tie her to the chair for all I care." With that, he grabbed his phone off the table and headed inside.

"You know what he's like," Jason said. "His sense of drama knows no bounds. I think that's why he likes you so much." Jason tried a smile.

"What's he going to do?" Charlie scratched her head.

Jason shrugged. "I have no earthly idea."

"I might as well stay. I have nowhere to go, anyway." Charlie drained the rest of her mimosa.

Discreetly, Jason pushed a basket with two croissants in her direction. Charlie grabbed one and started nibbling at it.

A few minutes later, Nick walked back out onto the terrace. "Here's what's going to happen," he announced. "Charlie, you're going to shower and make yourself presentable. Trust me, you want to do this." He gestured wildly with his hands. "After you've washed, Jason and I are going to the farmer's market. You're to wait here. I will not answer any questions. All I'm asking is that you trust me. I know trust is a big issue for you." He stretched his arms wide as though to physically display just how big an issue he thought it to be. "I'm your friend. I only want what's best for you. And I'm not the only one. Understood?" He sighed dramatically.

If she hadn't felt so foolish herself, Charlie would have wondered if Nick lived for moments like these. Regardless, she knew better than to argue with him. "Yes, Nickie."

"I will also call Ava and check up on her. I was as surprised as you were when she turned up at that auction, Charlie." He hung his head in disbelief. "How could you possibly have screwed that up? She made such a bold statement that night." He clasped his hands together. "Okay. In the shower you go."

"Can I finish my croissant first?" Charlie presented the pastry.

"Yes, yes, of course you can. Just don't dilly-dally."

* * *

After a shower cut short by Nick banging on the bathroom door, Charlie slipped into the one set of clothes left in her carry-on—she hadn't exactly packed for a lot of non-bedroom activities.

When she emerged from the guest room, Nick stood by the front door, checking his watch. "The bell's going to ring in about five minutes. Answer the door and please be polite. For once in your life, *listen*, Charlie." He opened his arms. "Come here."

Charlie hadn't been told what to do like this in a very long time. No one else could get away with it. She stepped into his embrace. He smelled the way he always did—clean and fresh. His beard scraped against Charlie's cheek. "Text when you're ready for us to come back, but take all the time you need."

Once they'd left, Charlie stared at the door for a few seconds. She wasn't born yesterday. Nick had called Jo. Anyone other and Nick wouldn't have required such a spectacle, but in a way, she was glad he had. It eased the nerves rising in her stomach, along with the fear she'd used as an excuse for putting off this inevitable moment for a very long time.

When the bell rang, right on time, Charlie was still startled by it.

She opened the door and looked at Jo standing in front of her.

"Hey, Charlie," she said. "Can I come in?"

"Of course." Charlie stepped aside. It was strange letting Jo into Nick and Jason's house, but she was glad to be on neutral territory to have this long-awaited conversation.

While Charlie was in the shower, Nick and Jason had tidied up the kitchen. "Not sure what I can offer you to drink." Charlie wiped her moist palms on her jeans. She hadn't offered to hug or even exchange a brief kiss on the cheek with her ex.

"I've got that covered." From a large bag slung over her shoulder, Jo produced a bottle of red wine. "Alex Duffy gave it to me, so it must be good."

From the way her fingers fiddled with the neck of the bottle, Charlie concluded that Jo was nervous too.

"Why don't you take it into the garden, and I'll be right out with two glasses." Charlie wasn't overly familiar with this kitchen, but she sure as hell knew where the wine glasses were located. She took the few moments alone to steel herself for what was to come. *Listen*, Nick had said. He was right, and she would do her best. What she wouldn't do was inquire about Christian or feel sorry about stealing time from him and Jo being together.

"It's so lovely here," Jo said when Charlie emerged from the house. She leaned her head back and basked in the midday sun. "I could get used to LA summers. And winters, I guess." She straightened her neck. "Remember when our AC broke in the middle of the hottest August in decades?"

How could Charlie ever forget? They'd just moved in together and the landlord had proved not very interested in maintaining his properties. She and Jo had slipped ice cubes into their bras and slept on top of the covers with all the windows open, the city noise a perfect soundtrack for those restless nights. "God, yes." When Charlie poured the wine, her hands trembled.

"Sorry for being such a lush last night."

"No need to apologize." Charlie sat down opposite her ex for the first time since she'd begged her—as good as on her knees—not to leave her for Christian. They'd exchanged text messages, spoken on the phone, and written e-mails, but after that last afternoon in their loft, Charlie had never been able to work up the nerve to face Jo. She'd been too angry at first. Then, simply too devastated. Afterward, she'd packed her things and moved to LA

"Just so you know, I was planning on getting in touch with you. It's silly for us to be in the same city and not see each other," Jo said. "I know you've had a hard time with… this, and I wanted to give you the space you so obviously needed." She swirled the wine in her glass. Maybe it was a bit early in the day for her. It wasn't for Charlie.

"I wasn't too pleased when Jason said you'd taken the job." Charlie took a sip. The wine was full-bodied and pleasant on the palate. "But I know it was a silly reaction. Just like last night, but that was… different. Partially, at least."

"It must have been hard seeing me and Christian sitting in Nickie and Jase's dining room like that. I'm sorry for what happened, although I don't know the details."

Charlie took another gulp. "I screwed up."

"You don't have to tell me, Charlie." At last, Jo drank. "But, if you're willing to listen, I would like to say a few things. Things I've been meaning to say for a long time but haven't gotten a chance to."

Charlie fixed her gaze on a tree branch to the left of Jo's face. It was hard to look directly at the woman who had broken her heart so thoroughly that Charlie had fled the city where they'd lived together. "Of course. Isn't that why you're here?"

"I haven't come here to argue or to open up old wounds. I'm simply here to talk and to tell you some things that, according to Nick, only I can tell you."

"Be my guest." Charlie couldn't keep a hint of sarcasm from creeping into her voice.

Jo sucked her bottom lip into her mouth the way she always did. The gesture didn't affect Charlie as much as she would have expected it to. "This isn't exactly easy for me either." She sat up a bit straighter in her chair. "Are you still so convinced that the only reason we broke up is because I fell in love with Christian?" Jo didn't mince her words.

Charlie shrugged as if it were just a rhetorical question.

"Charlie, come on." Jo's voice shot up a fraction. "I loved you for a very long time. Hell, I still love you, but you made it impossible for me to stay with you."

Charlie slumped in her chair.

Jo took another sip of wine, then tilted her head to the side. "This is what you do, Charlie. Exactly what you're doing right now."

"I'm not doing anything," Charlie said. She couldn't if she wanted to. All her muscles seemed to be suffering from a simultaneous cramp.

"It's hard to reason with *nothing*."

Charlie couldn't look at Jo. She wished Annie was here to offer some light distraction, but Nick and Jason had taken her to the market with them.

"Remember when we ran into Clara in Central Park, and all three of us went for a drink? You didn't speak to me for the rest of the day, Charlie. You gave me nothing, except the most agonizing, disapproving silence. Like you were such a big martyr, simply because you'd had to see me interact with my ex for an hour or so. Like you'd made the biggest sacrifice of your life for me."

Charlie opened her mouth, ready to launch into a defensive reply, but thought better of it. *There was obviously still something between you*, Charlie wanted to say. *Something that made me feel insignificant and terribly insecure.*

Jo shifted her weight in her chair and leaned over the table. "This is not the first time I'm telling you this, Charlie, so it shouldn't come as a shock. You have so much going for you. You're a terrific writer. I mean, look at you, living in Hollywood. You and I, we had some excellent times together, but sometimes I can't help but think that what you really excel at is self-sabotage. At not allowing yourself to be happy.

"The last year of our relationship, what you did more than anything was suck the joy out of everything for me. I didn't want to come home to you in the evening. You were always on edge, always suspicious and throwing around completely unfounded paranoia. You were unhappy. And you took it out on me."

Charlie couldn't hold in her accusation any longer. "Because you met someone else!" Her voice was high-pitched and full of blame.

Jo closed her eyes and shook her head, expelling a sigh. "My only hope for you, Charlie, was that you would have learned something from our breakup. I can understand—to expunge yourself from the biggest guilt—why you would fixate on that… fabricated truth, but I'd hoped you'd have come to your senses by now."

Charlie slammed the palm of her hand on the table. "For Christ's sake, Jo. Facts are facts. Did you or did you not fall in love with a—" Charlie stopped herself from saying the word 'man,' "someone else while we were still together?"

"Yes. I did. But have you ever really stopped to wonder why?" Jo planted her elbows on the table and curled her fingers tightly around the stem of her wineglass.

"Clearly, it was because I had somehow become the most awful person on the planet."

Jo sighed. "Here we go again. You're impossible to have a conversation with sometimes. You have such a big void to fill in your heart, you make everything about you. What about me? What about what I wanted?"

"It's very clear what you wanted."

"Fuck you, Charlie. If this is how you're going to be—if this is still the person you are—I want nothing to do with you." Jo pushed her chair back. "I advise you to take a long hard look in the mirror. The world is not against you, Charlie. All the other women on the planet are not here to plant a knife in your back, or to conspire against poor little Charlotte Cross who never did anything wrong in her life." The feet of her chair scraped against the terrace tiles as Jo pushed herself out of it. "Nobody's perfect, Charlie, least of all me. But neither are you." With that, Jo yanked her bag off the table and headed into the house. A few seconds later, the front door opened and then closed.

For several long moments, Charlie stared at the empty space where Jo had sat. It was familiar territory, after all.

CHAPTER TWENTY-TWO

Instead of looking at herself in the mirror, Charlie went up to the Griffith Park Observatory and stared at the Hollywood sign. Ever since she'd seen it on TV as a young girl, she'd felt that twinge of desire to be part of this mythical place. Now she was. Although the real reason why she'd come here—fled here—wasn't very glamorous.

It was late afternoon, and apart from a few bites of croissant, Charlie hadn't eaten anything. She wasn't tipsy, but she probably shouldn't have driven anywhere. She sat in a secluded spot and just gazed, feeling exactly the same way she had when she'd first arrived. In awe of where she'd ended up, despite herself, and still so terribly out of place. But perhaps this city *was* where she belonged. If only for its reputation of inhabitants who attached much more importance to what lay on the surface than to what really mattered.

Here, Charlie could pretend. Or at least *try* to pretend. But she'd ended up in the exact same position as before. Alone. And terribly, madly in love with a woman she had expertly chased away. She stared at the sign again. This was not how it was supposed to feel when all her dreams came true.

She'd written *Crying Rivers* for Robin, who had also left her, and she'd cringed when Ava had wanted to read a paragraph out loud. Those few sentences she'd produced so long ago—and believed in so much—

seemed so far removed from how she felt now. Charlie could only dream of being able to say those words out loud again and, along with it, experience the sentiment they evoked. Hope. Happiness. A sense of stability she'd lost since Jo left her.

Because why did it always have to go exactly the same way? Why couldn't Charlie be the Charlie she so desperately wanted to be—someone dependable. A woman secure enough in herself she didn't have to worry about percentages, and succumb to self-destructive bursts of jealousy. She hashed over Liz's words. "We all have many faults." And whereas Charlie didn't have the slightest issue cataloging most of her own, she was very adept at forgiving others theirs. Except when, as in Ava's case, she could fabricate and mold them, and turn them into something she could use to refuse herself happiness.

Charlie was well aware she was her own worst enemy. She hadn't always been this way. And when she really thought about it and asked herself when she had last been so exquisitely happy, so reeling with joy because of something she herself had accomplished, as opposed to when she'd experienced happiness because of Ava kissing her on the beach, or bidding on her at the auction, it was when she'd typed 'The End' after finishing *Crying Rivers*. Charlie had prided herself on never craving any sort of mind-altering substance like drugs or alcohol, because she had something at her disposal with a much more powerful, a much more long-lasting, profound effect. She had writing.

First and foremost, Charlie was a writer and nothing—nothing!—came close to that indescribable feeling of committing words to paper, to creating a world that hadn't existed before she dreamed it up, to the magic sensation of words, sentences, and paragraphs, as they flowed from her fingers and onto the page. And, if she was completely honest with herself, she missed it so much, because it was such a large part of who she was. As exciting as Hollywood could be, as thrilling as it had been to sign that television deal for *Underground*, it also profoundly disturbed her equilibrium. Charlie, she could see now, had lost herself. She hadn't allowed herself to heal after the breakup from Jo. Instead, she'd run away to this glamorous city, where she spent the better part of her day in a room with other people. It was not who Charlie was.

She thought about *Crying Rivers* again, the book that had changed everything. About that particular paragraph that had summed up her journey and the words she craved to be able to apply to herself once again.

Charlie didn't need to read them from a page. She knew them because the words were still *in* her heart somewhere. But, after all this renewed heartache, she still hadn't managed to learn from her mistakes. Maybe it was time.

She closed her eyes, the sight of the Hollywood sign now almost too heavy a burden, and images of Jo storming off, and Ava saying that if Charlie left now, they'd be well and truly over, combined into an unbearable storm of guilt in her mind.

Charlie wasn't so obtuse she couldn't see the truth in what Jo had said. But it was hard to admit, because if Jo was right, that made the rules Charlie had made up and lived by obsolete. Complete and utter nonsense. That a woman like Ava had even given her the time of day after Charlie had mentioned it was almost unfathomable.

Then Charlie allowed herself to remember another something Jo had said. On that day she'd confirmed Charlie's suspicions about her and Christian, and had left her.

"When will you realize you're worth it, Charlie? That you're just as worthy of being loved as the next person. When will you stop ruining your relationships because you're convinced that you're not lovable? When will you snap out of that destructive self-fulfilling prophecy?"

When Charlie opened her eyes and looked into the brightness of a Los Angeles Sunday afternoon, tears were streaming down her cheeks, and she had two urgent matters to attend to. She had to apologize to Jo. And she had to send a clear message to Ava.

She dug her phone out of her pocket, wiped most of the tears from her face, and switched on the camera function. She had dark circles under her eyes, and the eyes Jo and Robin had always praised as the most beautiful blue were filled with regret, fear, and, most of all, sadness she'd caused herself. It was time to stop clinging to silly rules and giving in to unfounded jealousy. She needed to look past her own woes and pay more attention to what others wanted.

Charlie couldn't compete with Ava's grand gesture of turning up at the auction and declaring her interest in Charlie so audaciously. But she knew what she could do, what she *had* to do. She took a deep breath and started reciting the words she hadn't been able to say or hear out loud since Jo had left her.

* * *

Charlie stopped at an In-n-Out Burger on her way back to WeHo. It reminded her of how Ava could display such joy while eating, and how very un-model-like and un-LA she was about food. So many things about Los Angeles didn't agree with the view she'd had of the city for the longest time. For once, she didn't fail to see how she'd made a habit of indulging in thoughts like that, sometimes for the perceived sake of self-protection, but more often than not out of sheer stubbornness and her desire to cling to ideas she had believed in for so long.

She parked outside of her house but didn't go in. Instead, she called Jo, who didn't pick up. Charlie left a message with a brief apology and a request to redeem herself for her outburst earlier. Instead of going inside her home—a place that represented a loneliness Charlie still couldn't face—she walked to Lux. With luck, some of her softball team members might be hanging out.

"You're back early." Liz checked her watch. "Are you that excited about tomorrow that you took an earlier flight?" She quirked up one eyebrow.

"Oh, Lizzie." Charlie pulled up a chair. "Why have you never told me I'm such a navel-gazing asshole?"

"Because you're not, you silly woman." Without asking, Liz poured Charlie a glass from the pitcher of beer on the table.

Charlie greeted a few other team members. Josie sat at the adjoining table, her hand draped over another girl's knee. If Josie noticed her at all, she didn't show it.

"How's life in the land of grand gestures and glamorous TV hosts?" Tiff asked. "I thought you'd be done playing with us now that you've slept your way up to the big leagues."

"Lay off, Tiff," Liz said.

"It fucking sucks," Charlie replied, even though Tiff was just teasing. "I missed you ladies so much, I climbed down from my high and mighty pedestal to drink humble beer with you."

"Words are not enough," Tiff said. "I want to see you at practice on Wednesday and in a team jersey on Sunday."

"At your service, boss." Charlie saluted Tiff military-style. "I may even try to actually hit a ball next game."

"Big words, Charlie, big words," Tiff said. "Way to raise expectations."

A few more girls joined in on their gentle verbal

sparring match, and Charlie sank a bit deeper into her chair, safe in the knowledge that she was among friends.

CHAPTER TWENTY-THREE

Charlie didn't feel completely at ease having to conduct this conversation in front of Christian, but she had to accept him as a part of Jo's life at some point, so she may as well start now.

"I want you to see, Charlie," Jo had said, "that Christian is not the devil reincarnated. He didn't steal me from you. He is, in fact, an awesome dude, whom I think, if you're in any way serious about apologizing to me and having me in your life, you should make an effort to get to know better."

Eleven months of apprehension don't just dissolve because of good intentions, but Charlie decided to make the effort instead of indulging in her irrational disgust with straight guys. It was true that she didn't know Christian and that, in her head, she'd only ever allowed him to grow into more and more of a monster as time passed.

Christian was a bearded man with a booming, confident voice. He wasn't overly tall, but had broad shoulders that tapered into a slim waistline. Of course, he wore skinny jeans. The first few months after the breakup, Charlie refused to refer to him in any other way than "the fucking bearded hipster." Heavy emphasis on the f-word every time.

He and Jo lounged on the sidewalk terrace of one of WeHo's many coffee houses. Despite the pair of them being full-blooded New Yorkers, they looked as though they firmly belonged. Jo had tied her unruly mane of curly hair together in a lush ponytail, and it occurred to Charlie as she sat down opposite them—ready to nail herself to the cross for her mistakes—that they looked good together. As though put on this earth for each other.

The realization stung.

For weeks, Charlie had fallen into a miserable sort of half sleep with nothing but images of Christian's big man hands all over Jo, his beard chafing her soft cheeks.

He pushed himself lightly out of his seat as Charlie sat down, like the gentleman Charlie refused to believe he might be. He'd gone after someone who was already taken, after all. He extended his hand, and this time, Charlie shook it without prompting.

"How was the big love shoot?" Jo asked, after pecking Charlie quickly on the cheek. "Nick told me all about it."

"It was something else." Charlie looked into Jo's dark eyes and remembered how she'd based the physical appearance of the *Underground* heroine on her ex.

"Is this how you want me to look?" Jo had asked once, when Charlie described Aretha as having a very muscular frame. "Is this your way of telling me I should spend more time in the gym?" They'd laughed about it then, and Charlie had stroked Jo's biceps and told her how perfect they were and how she shouldn't try to match up to fictional characters. Charlie had started writing *Underground* not long after she and Jo had gotten together.

"So Aretha, who, we both know is entirely based on me," Jo said, a silly grin on her face, "is portrayed by Elisa Fox. I suppose I could have done worse." She jabbed Christian in the upper arm.

"I never got the chance to congratulate you on all of this, Charlie," he said, as if that prod against his arm was

Jo's cue for him to say this. But Charlie had made a few wrong assumptions about Jo and Christian before, and decided to not get on her high horse yet. He was complimenting her, after all.

"Thanks. It's a bit surreal."

"A bit surreal? Isn't it what you've always dreamed of, Charlie?" Jo said. "I'm so, so proud of you."

"Yeah well, I guess I can't screw everything up." She gave them a shy grimace. This was as good a time as any to launch into that apology. "I'm sorry about the other day, Jo. I should have been more... open-minded. I see that now."

"Charlie," Christian said. "I really need you to know that nothing happened between Jo and me until after you'd broken up. We were friends for a long time before..." Thankfully, he stopped there.

"Hey, Charlie Cross," a woman's voice came from behind Charlie. "Where's Ava Castaneda? Way to go, girl!"

Charlie turned to the side to find a woman in her early twenties giving her the thumbs-up. Charlie nodded and looked away. Luckily, the woman went on her way and left Charlie alone.

Jo stretched her arm over the table and found Charlie's hand. "That must make you so uncomfortable. I know you, Charlie. You're dying a little bit inside right now." Jo's gesture was so sweet, so Jo, and such a throwback to their happier times together, Charlie did, in fact, crumble a little on the inside. Not because she was mortified about being recognized as Ava's girlfriend when she no longer was, but because Jo's heart was on display.

She shrugged. "I'm sure the news that it's all over before it even began will spread soon enough."

Jo didn't say anything, and Christian scooped some milk foam out of his coffee cup. Charlie took it as an open invitation to tell them what had happened, but she could only deal with one heartbreak at a time. "I screwed that up as well, but I'm trying to make amends there, too."

Charlie hadn't heard from Ava since she'd sent her the video two days ago. No acknowledgement of receipt. Nothing. For all Charlie knew, Eric had gotten his way and had made a successful move on a hurt and angry Ava. Although she tried very, very hard not to let her thoughts wander in that direction too much.

"I don't need you to apologize to me," Jo said. "I just need you to see that you and I drifted apart long before our relationship ended."

Christian shuffled in his chair nervously, then pushed it back. "I'm going to find the bathroom," he said.

Jo nodded and followed him with her gaze as he made his way inside. "He didn't really want to come. I made him. More for moral support than anything else, I guess."

"I *do* see." Charlie pulled her hand from underneath Jo's and started tugging at her fingertips.

Jo put her hand back on Charlie's. "I'm not sitting here with the illusion that one conversation can instantly turn us from estranged exes into friends, but I'm going to be in LA for a few more months, and I would like to use that time to make things better between us. I need for that to happen. You aren't just a memory for me, Charlie. We had so much between us…" Her voice cracked.

Charlie's throat swelled with sudden dryness. She could only nod.

"I know you're too smart to really believe we broke up over a guy," Jo added. "It was over long before I met Christian."

Charlie stopped a tear from dropping from the corner of her eye. "For the longest time, I couldn't wrap my head around it, Jo… My thoughts oscillated between being convinced you left me because you weren't into women in the first place and thinking that I must have really done a number on you to make you go off women and flee into the arms of a man. Even though I know now I was just fooling myself with both assumptions."

"You're in your head so much of the time. You make a living out of making things up." Jo curled her lips into a small smile. "When are you going to write something new, by the way?"

Charlie grabbed a napkin. "Maybe it is time for a follow-up to *Crying Rivers*."

"Make it a happy one." Jo leaned back a bit. "I can't take another tearjerker like that."

"There was so much truth in that book, though. No wonder I avoided any mention or thought of it after you and I parted ways. *Underground* being picked up also gave me the perfect excuse to pretend I wasn't who I was."

"I think you should do it, Charlie. Write the book."

"My getting-over-you book?" Charlie attempted a grin. "Are you jealous because Robin has one dedicated to her and you don't?"

Jo squeezed Charlie's hand. "I think I have a right to it," she joked. "Seven years with Charlie Cross should have at least earned me that."

Charlie stifled a chuckle, then cleared her throat. "When did you fall out of love with me?"

Jo huffed some air out of her nostrils. "I never did. You fell out of love with yourself."

Charlie pulled up an eyebrow. "What are you talking about? I'm fucking amazing." It came out as a whisper full of irony.

"In all earnestness. Not long after our sixth anniversary, just after the rights to *Underground* had been sold, something changed. I don't know if it was because dealing with Hollywood pushed you out of your comfort zone, or if it was something between us. All I know is that I didn't change, but you slowly slipped away from me, and I tried and I tried, but there was nothing I could do to make you snap out of it. You sort of shut down. You stopped trusting me, I know that much. And when you looked to the future, it always felt as though there was no room in that picture for me. It may seem as though I'm the one who hurt you by leaving, but you hurt me, too, Charlie. Deeply."

"I'm sorry." Charlie was truly sniveling now.

"I've moved on. I'm happy with Christian. But you, Charlie, you're such a mess."

Charlie withdrew her hand from the table and tried to catch some of her tears. She hoped Christian wasn't about to make his return to the table. She didn't want him to see her this way. Not to mention she was in public. So far, only one person had addressed her, but surely more recognized her. A paparazzi might be skulking behind some trees down the road, his ultra-zoom lens aimed at her like the barrel of a gun.

"Oh, fuck it." Through her tears, Charlie gazed at Jo. She was crying, too. "Maybe we shouldn't have done this here."

"My bad." Jo produced a packet of tissues from her purse and offered one to Charlie. "I think Christian went for a stroll around the block." She managed a chuckle. "The fact of the matter is, Charlie, I don't want to keep on pretending you never existed to ignore the pain of our breakup. If anything, I would like you to be part of my life again."

"It *has* been almost a year." Charlie dabbed her eyes with the tissue. "I suppose we can give it a go."

"Thank goodness." A more forceful smile broke on Jo's face. "You're not easy to ignore in this town, you know?"

"I'm just a writer." Charlie stretched her legs under

the table and her knee briefly touched Jo's. "Bottom of the food chain in Hollywood."

"Are you truly happy with what you're doing here? Your life must be night and day compared to what it was in New York." Under the table, Jo didn't pull her leg away.

"It's exciting and crazy, and takes a shitload of energy from me every single day," Charlie replied.

"Always a master at dodging questions." Jo tapped her calf against Charlie's shin. "Are you happy?" she asked, again.

"I might be… if I can get Ava to talk to me again."

Jo cocked her head, indicating she was not satisfied with that reply.

"And once we wrap filming and I start writing again."

Jo exhaled a sigh of relief. "Hallelujah." She continued to let her knee rest against Charlie. "I believe I know you pretty well, Charlie. And you were never happier than when you'd finished a productive writing day. Just you, your computer, the characters in your head, and a window to look out of."

"And you coming home to me in the evening." Charlie banged her knee playfully against Jo's.

"For a while, that was enough." A solemn expression took over her face. "Until Hollywood called."

CHAPTER TWENTY-FOUR

"If you look at your watch one more time, I think it might disintegrate from your relentless woeful stares," Liz said.

Charlie sighed. It had been ten days since she'd sent that video to Ava, and she still hadn't heard anything back. Nick claimed he'd barely been able to get in touch with her, either. Ava and the *Knives Out* crew were due back in LA that day, and Charlie was worried.

"Still no news?" Liz asked.

"Nothing. It's like she's gone on a total social media hiatus as well. Nothing on Instagram or Pinterest. In this day and age…"

"It could just be that she's licking her wounds."

"Or sleeping with Eric Brunswick."

Liz shook her head. "Not to throw salt in your wound, Charlotte, but I need to head home. It's our wedding anniversary."

"For real?" They'd gone for a quick drink after the day's shoot had wrapped. "Then why are you sitting here with me?"

"I believe it's called friendship." Liz rose. "And Sarah had to work late." She threw in a casual smile.

"Say hello to your better half from me. Tell her she put a ring on a good one."

"Will do. What are you up to tonight?"

"Revise tomorrow's scripts. Look at today's rushes and make sure the dialogue flows well. Perhaps finally start plotting my next novel."

"Don't forget to relax, Charlie." Liz squeezed her shoulder. "She'll be in touch soon. I'm sure of it."

Liz walked away. Charlie wasn't so sure Liz was right. Ava had no reason to ever contact her again. Charlie had spent a lot of time putting herself in Ava's shoes, and the conclusion had been evident. Still, now that Ava was headed back to LA—or was perhaps already here—a sparkle of hope stayed stubbornly lodged in the back of her brain. Nevertheless, a video could only accomplish so much. Perhaps a face-to-face meeting could kick-start... something. Though Charlie wasn't sure what.

Charlie lost herself in daydreams and plans to somehow convince Ava that she'd been infinitely stupid to let Eric get under her skin, that she'd been cruel to not take Ava's feelings into consideration more, and that she'd basically repeated all her past mistakes. She was so caught up in her thoughts that she didn't notice the grey BMW parked on her street.

She was already putting the key into the lock of her front door when the car registered as being the exact same make, model, and color as the one Ava drove. Charlie headed back onto the street to check the vehicle out again. As soon as her gaze landed on it, the door opened, and a leg appeared from the driver's side. A long, long leg with an elegant foot shoed in a glossy black flat.

Charlie's heart started drumming, the vibration creating a sizzle under her skin.

"Hey, you." Ava stood three feet away from her. "I thought you'd never get home."

Charlie smiled. Her heart beat so quickly, she feared it might burst out of her chest. Ava took a step closer, and Charlie blurted, "Most people call first these days."

"What can I say?" Ava stepped closer still. "I guess I'm an old-fashioned girl."

"Do you want to come in?" It was the polite thing to say.

Ava hoisted her bag over her shoulder and locked her car with the push of a button on the key fob. "I think that would be best."

Charlie let them both in. Ava's presence in her house was unsettling, but also energizing and nerve-wracking. "Glass of Pinot?" Charlie asked.

"Just water, please. I'm driving." Ava looked around the living room as though it was the first time she set foot in the place. She'd only been to Charlie's house twice before, and they hadn't spent a lot of time discussing the interior design.

Charlie grabbed them a couple of bottles of water from the fridge and invited Ava to sit. As soon as she did, Ava opened her purse and unearthed her copy of *Crying Rivers*. With a dramatic bang, she deposited it on the coffee table between them.

Charlie stared at it, unsure of what was expected from her. She cut her eyes to Ava, who'd folded one leg over the other, looking incredibly delicious in jeans and a simple white T-shirt. It made a few of Charlie's body parts ache.

"I want you to read it to me, Charlie. Here and now." She pursed her lips for a moment. "I can't make any promises as to what it will or will not result in, but I think it's a good place to start."

Charlie's throat went dry. She reached for her water and took a few sips. She'd recited the words out loud, and by heart, for the video she sent Ava. There was no reason she couldn't do it in the safety of her own home with Ava sitting directly across from her. Charlie forced herself to rise to the occasion and straightened her spine. "Okay." She looked at the cover of her breakthrough novel. It was understated, unlike its contents, with a blue river winding its way up into a pinkbled sky, her name positioned at the bottom in big bulky letters. The title font was curvy and white. Such a simple cover for such a desperate book. The book that had fallen straight from Charlie's heart onto the page. She hadn't written anything of the sort since then. Soon after she'd finished *Crying Rivers*, she'd met Jo, and started on the *Underground* series. The rest was history. Maybe Jo had been right. Maybe Charlie had to confront all her fears, dashed hopes, and expectations on the page again. Maybe it was the only way.

Then she started. "When I re-emerged from the ashes of my former life and examined the scar on my hand, a remnant from when I had broken a wine glass out of pure rage after she left, and saw how it had healed itself through a magical process—a process called time— I knew this had happened to my heart as well. I realized that what I had so adamantly believed my heart to be incapable of, had in fact occurred—while I was unaware. While I was living. And this time, when I cried, it wasn't a river, just a single tear sliding from the corner of my eye across my cheek, and it was born from a happiness I had been convinced I would be denied forever."

As she spoke the last sentence, a tear dangled from Charlie's eyelashes, and dripped onto her hands.

"I knew you could do it, Charlie. I knew when I wanted to read it for you that time in my house."

Now that she'd read it out loud, and the emotions of the time when she'd written those words came over her again, Charlie couldn't do anything but sit in her spot stiffly and let sadness wash over her. But inertia and self-pity weren't going to get her Ava back.

"I'm sorry for what happened in Dallas. I should have known better. I shouldn't have given in to my delusions. I should have been stronger. For you." Charlie let the tears stream and didn't bother wiping them from her cheeks. "You have no idea how sorry I am, Ava."

"I think I do. But this isn't about how sorry you

are." Ava unfolded her legs and crossed them at the ankle. She grabbed the book off the table and leafed through the pages with her thumb. "I asked you to stay, Charlie. Practically begged you. And you left, anyway. That's twice now that you've discarded me to go and feel sorry for yourself. It doesn't make for a very stable basis for any sort of relationship. Not friendship, and definitely not *more* than friendship."

Charlie nodded. She understood, but more than that, now was the time to fight. Ava had come here when she could just as easily not have bothered. She must have some feelings left for Charlie.

"Some things have happened since I fled Dallas. I wouldn't call it a breakdown, but it wasn't far off either." Charlie fixed her gaze on Ava. "I had a confrontation with my ex and a series of… I guess you could call them epiphanies." The tears stopped leaking from Charlie's eyes. "Meeting you and seeing Jo again has finally lifted that blanket of self-pity and fear I'd wrapped myself in. When I met you, I wasn't ready. But I know I am now. Perhaps I don't deserve another chance, but I think you should give me one, anyway." Charlie pursed her lips into the start of a smile. "You wouldn't be here if you didn't have even the slightest hint of desire to try again."

Ava tipped her head to the side briefly. "These are all words, though. You can record me a video, even write me the most heartfelt letter. They would all just be words. Words I've heard before. What would truly change? Not just in word, but also in deed?"

"I'm going back to who I truly am. To what made me into the person I am today. A person with many faults, granted, but one with better qualities as well. I'm going back to the one thing on this planet that connects my heart, my true feelings, with everything and everyone around me. I'm going to start on my next novel."

"The next volume in the *Underground* series?" Ava

didn't sound very impressed.

"No." Charlie's voice was loud and undeniable. "The next *Crying Rivers.*"

Ava narrowed her eyes. "What about the reason why you're in Hollywood in the first place?"

"That's not what will make me stay. You see, there's this woman I can't get out of my head. She's gorgeous, and kind, and smart, and she believes in second *and* third chances."

"Does she now?"

"I'm convinced she does." Charlie allowed a full smile to break on her face. "I truly am."

"Are you sure she's not just a character you made up for one of your novels?"

Charlie shook her head. "No, but I am sure she'll make an appearance in my next one. Based on a true character."

"Does this 'woman' have any more good qualities?" Ava's cheeks dimpled.

"She does, although she does have a questionable sense of humor. But she has great taste in real estate. She isn't afraid to make a bold move. She's also the most beautiful woman I, personally, have ever met in my life. And the things she can do with her fingers…"

Ava let out a chuckle. Charlie could tell she hadn't meant to laugh like that.

"Most of all, though," Charlie continued, "this woman knows compassion. And she isn't afraid, like others, to follow her heart, no matter who it leads her to."

"Is this woman about to stand up, ask the same of you, and kiss you?" Ava pushed herself out of the sofa.

"Yes." Charlie followed her example.

"I think you forgot to say that this woman is also wise beyond her years—years of which there are no visible signs whatsoever on her face or other body parts—and who deserves to have all her wishes obeyed from now until further notice." Ava took a pace sideways and stood next to the coffee table.

"It's true that this woman can get carried away at times. But, despite being spoiled and pampered from a young age because of her extraordinary looks, this woman has been able to maintain a sense of balance and not grow too massive an ego."

"This woman sounds like such a fucking catch, Charlie."

Charlie's resolve finally broke and she rushed to Ava's side. "You have no idea." Charlie folded her arms around Ava's waist.

"You'd better not be foolish enough to let go of her again." Ava stared down at her.

"Never." Charlie pressed her body against Ava's and rested her head on her shoulder.

"I believe the woman asked for a kiss," Ava whispered in her ear.

Charlie looked up. Ava's scent surrounded her, her arms rested on her shoulders, her hair tickled her neck. "If I remember correctly the woman asked for much more than that."

They both broke out in a giggle. Tension seeped from Charlie's muscles. She gazed into Ava's eyes.

"The woman most certainly did." Ava grinned madly at her. "But first things first." She slanted her head and kissed her.

CHAPTER TWENTY-FIVE

"Charlie, wake up." Still drowsy with sleep, Charlie forced one eye open. Instantly, a smile burst on her lips at the sight of the person looking back at her. "Today's the day, Charlie."

"Jesus. What time is it?" Charlie couldn't care less about the time. It was Sunday and that was all she needed to know.

"I don't think you understand." Ava trailed two fingertips up Charlie's chest underneath the sheets. "We have no time to waste here." Her fingers reached Charlie's nipple and squeezed.

"Ouch." Over the covers, Charlie grabbed hold of Ava's assaulting hand. "Some of us were up half the night. It wasn't you, Snoring Beauty."

"You'd better take that back." Ava's fingers stiffened underneath the sheets, and she managed to flatten her hand against her breast. "And if you think that's going to stop me, you don't know me very well." Ava slipped on top of her and started tugging down the sheets, baring Charlie's chest. "How many times a week do you work out, Charlie? Because I'm in the gym almost every day." Ava demonstrated her strength by curling her fingers around Charlie's wrists and pinning them above her head. She was naked as well and her nipples caressed the skin of Charlie's belly. "I'll give you some respite if you tell me the first sentence of your new book is about me." Ava smiled down at her.

"You can't ask me that. It breaks the magic of the first draft."

"Bullshit." Ava shifted her weight forward and brushed a nipple across Charlie's lips, then quickly pulled away.

"I just can't win with you." Charlie sagged back into the pillows, secretly relishing the firm grip Ava had on her wrists. Because of the power she was exerting, her biceps popped, and her clavicle appeared more inviting to lick than ever. "You don't play fair."

"I'll show you how fair I am." Ava narrowed her eyes and the skin around them crinkled. She leaned over and kissed Charlie on the nose first, then firmly on the lips. The kiss quickly transformed into a deeper one, and when Ava slipped her tongue out of Charlie's mouth, she was breathing heavily. "I want you, Charlie Cross, that's all."

Ava let go of Charlie's wrists and lay down beside her, yanking most of the sheets off Charlie in the process. "Did you have a good start?"

"Very." Charlie found Ava's hand with hers and interlaced their fingers. "That improvised writing desk you set up for me is very inspiring."

"I'm glad." Ava rested her head next to Charlie's and pressed a kiss to her cheek, then her temple.

Charlie pulled their intertwined hands to her mouth and kissed the back of Ava's hand. "I can't believe you actually woke me up for this."

"Because of your neurotic antics, we missed a lot of precious time together. It's only fair that you make up for that by sleeping less." Ava's breath was hot on Charlie's cheek. "And what I'm asking of you is hardly punishment."

Charlie's skin broke out in gooseflesh at the thought of what Ava was asking of her. "You're not even going to make me breakfast first?" Charlie wasn't the least bit interested in breakfast. She'd barely eaten since Ava had turned up on her doorstep last Thursday. Her stomach was wholly upturned by butterflies.

"Why are you stalling, Charlie? Are you nervous?" Amusement shone through in Ava's voice.

Hell no, Charlie wanted to say, but decided to be truthful instead. "A little, I guess."

"That's so sweet and adorable."

Sweet and adorable were not words Charlie wanted associated with what she was about to do. "We'll see about that," she said, and started to slide away from Ava. "You stay here. Don't move an inch." Charlie got out of bed and regarded Ava. Judging by how silent she had fallen, she was ready for what would happen next—so ready she'd woken Charlie up for it.

Charlie grabbed the harness they'd examined extensively together the day before and disappeared into the bathroom.

She and Ava had gone over the instructions together—and it wasn't all that difficult. But Charlie hadn't done this in a very long time, and she had to brace herself, hands on the sides of the wash basin, and take a few deep breaths. There would only be one day in her life when she'd fuck Ava this way for the very first time.

At last, Charlie took another good look at the straps and the dildo. It had traveled quite a distance already and finally come all this way—just like Charlie. She maneuvered herself into it, tightening the straps around her buttocks, the silicone toy standing proud between her legs. Despite the sense of power it gave her, Charlie had to mumble a few words of encouragement to herself. To show herself like this to a new lover was highly intimate. The addition of a toy always demanded an increased level of trust and abandon.

Charlie stepped back into the bedroom. Ava lay on her side, her elbow propped underneath her, her head resting in her palm. At the sight of Charlie all strapped-on, her eyes widened. As a manner of invitation, she threw the sheets to one side. Charlie walked to the bed at a solemn pace, the toy dangling between her legs. When she climbed on, Ava came for her instantly, bringing her hands to Charlie's neck, pulling her close.

"You walking over here is one of the hottest things I've ever seen," she whispered, before kissing Charlie. There was nothing slow or tentative about this kiss. It was all intent and probing tongues and pulling Charlie as close as possible by the back of her neck. There was no doubt as to exactly how much Ava wanted this. Funny how Charlie had believed it would be the other way around. Now, sitting here with Ava's hands all over her, she couldn't imagine it any other way.

Charlie pushed Ava down onto her back. No more words were needed now. She sat naked with nothing but a dildo strapped to her loins. Beneath the panel of the fabric keeping it all together, her clit pulsed along with her heart. Even when she'd finally allowed herself to indulge in images of her and Ava together, this particular scene had been off limits. Charlie hadn't dared to dream this boldly. She hadn't dared to do a lot of things.

But here she was, in Ava's bed, the ocean outside ebbing away for the low morning tide, Ava looking up at her with lust in her eyes. No wonder Charlie hadn't yet experienced the overwhelming sensation of all her dreams coming true since arriving in LA. *This* was the only dream that mattered. She was worthy, and she was ready. And she had Ava by her side.

Charlie lay down next Ava and kissed her. Their lips met again and again in a frantic, charged connection of mouths and tongues. The dildo was lodged between their upper thighs, and the feel of it against her skin made Charlie's flesh sizzle.

"Fuck me, Charlie," Ava said when they broke from

their kiss. "God, please, fuck me."

A wicked grin spread over Charlie's lips. She remembered how Ava had teased her the very first time she'd been in her bedroom, how she'd made her wait for it. It was Charlie's intention to do exactly the same. She wanted it all now, wanted to explore every nook and cranny of Ava's body, drive her completely crazy before giving her what she wanted.

"Why don't you turn around," Charlie said. It wasn't a question.

Ava responded with a prolonged stare into Charlie's eyes, before turning on her belly, her arms slipping underneath the pillow she rested her head on.

Charlie gasped at the image of beauty displayed before her eyes. Ava's dark skin looked scrumptious against the cream sheets. Her back flowed into her behind in a sensual curve. Without thinking, Charlie extended her hand and stroked Ava's smooth skin. At first, she used only her fingertips and let them skate over the soft expanse lightly, creating a field of goose flesh in their wake, but soon, Charlie couldn't resist and caressed Ava with her full hand. By the time she'd dragged it all the way up Ava's legs, she was kneading, her own arousal and impatience reflected in her actions.

Charlie wanted this just as much as Ava—if not more. Making her wait wasn't an easy task. She planted her hands on either side of Ava's back and lowered herself until her body was flush against Ava's. The length of the dildo pressed into the soft flesh of Ava's behind. Charlie kissed her neck, her shoulders, and slowly made her way down, until her lips reached the curve of her ass. Charlie bared her teeth and sank them into Ava's behind gently. Beneath her, Ava squirmed with delight and, surely, impatience.

As lovely as Ava's backside was, Charlie had to see her face. "Turn back around," she asked, a much more pleading tone in her voice than when she'd asked the first time.

"I've been awake for hours, Charlie." Ava reached out her hands and pulled Charlie to her. "Thinking about this. I'm ready." There was urgency in her voice—need. Their lips met again and Ava's tongue was hot and slippery in Charlie's mouth, making her resolve crumble. She would need more time to learn to say no to this woman. Or at least, not yet. Charlie let her hand roam across Ava's skin, her fingers searching out her nipples. She wanted to play with them for hours, take them into her mouth, gaze at the perfect roundness of Ava's breasts, etch their shape into her memory forever, but her pulse was ever-quickening, her pussy swollen against the strap-on harness.

"Fuck me," Ava repeated. The way she said it made Charlie's head spin a little.

Charlie pushed herself onto her knees and took a short moment to revel in the beauty of Ava's body. Her hands lay draped above her head, her chest completely exposed. The ease with which she offered her body to Charlie set her blood on fire. Most exciting of all, however, was the look in Ava's eyes. It was demanding and vulnerable at the same time. It was the look of a woman Charlie never wanted to disappoint again. Ava Castaneda, the woman who compelled Charlie to find herself again.

Charlie kissed Ava's nipple, her hand grabbing for the other one. Intoxication overtook her. She was inebriated with raw lust for Ava. Charlie let her body take control. Her one hand squeezed while her tongue flicked Ava's nipple. Then, Charlie felt a hand on hers. A hand that pushed hers down. Ava forced it down as far as she could. Her legs were spread wide. Charlie propped herself up a bit and looked into Ava's eyes. The same pleading look of need shone in them. Charlie let her hand drift lower, over Ava's pubic hair, to the wetness pooling between her legs.

She gasped when she discovered how wet Ava was for her, how ready. Charlie darted her fingers over Ava's soaked sex. It was all softness and arousal and desire. Juices soon coated her fingertips. She locked her gaze on Ava's, and slipped two fingers inside.

Ava's muscles tensed instantaneously, but Charlie was still sitting next to her, and her position was not right. She gave Ava one more deep stroke, her own body tensing at the feel of all this warm, slick body, then retreated.

"Oh, Christ," Ava moaned. Her hands were above her head again, her features drawn into an expression of pure agony. "You're such a tease."

Charlie tried to ignore Ava's pleading and moved between her legs. The tip of the toy touched Ava's upper thigh, and it was enough to make her writhe underneath Charlie's gaze. But Charlie wanted to do something else first. She needed to taste. She lowered her head to Ava's pussy, inhaled her scent, and kissed the spot right next to her clit, then traced a path along Ava's drenched, puffed-up lips, let her tongue slip inside, until, finally, she dragged it up to Ava's clit again, and licked before sucking it into her mouth.

Ava moaned louder and Charlie needed to stop. Reluctantly, she pulled away from Ava's pussy. Charlie cupped some of Ava's juices in the palm of her hand and stroked them along the shaft of the dildo. She inched close enough to let the tip skate along Ava's lips and gave her clit a quick nudge with it.

"Oh, God." Ava moaned. "Please, Charlie, please."

Delighted by the moment, Charlie acquiesced. She shifted her weight forward, and, slowly, pushed the dildo inside of Ava. The sight of the pink toy disappearing between Ava's lips made Charlie's mouth go dry. Her heart hammered in her chest.

"Oh, yes," Ava said. "Oh, yes, Charlie. Fuck me." Ava's voice was a low whimper, insistent but quiet.

Half inside, Charlie changed position, draping herself over Ava's body. The choice between watching the dildo enter Ava's pussy or the enchantment on Ava's face from close up was an easy one for Charlie to make. She thrust into Ava, slow and gentle at first, and every time she pushed forward, her clit met the panel of the harness.

Charlie had watched Ava on TV for years. She'd seen her enjoy food, put on a serious face when she had to eliminate a contestant, and celebrate when a winner was announced. None of Ava's TV faces came close to how her features contorted in a mask of pleasure, a study in the focus of ecstasy, a display so utterly beautiful and arousing, Charlie believed she might very well come just at the sight of it.

Ava had brought her hands to Charlie's back and dug her nails in deep. Then, Ava pulled up her legs, and folded them across Charlie's lower back, and Charlie felt so extremely close to her—such a stark contrast to how far she had removed herself emotionally from Ava to protect her wounded ego.

Charlie increased the pace and force of her strokes. Ava drew a heavy breath, head thrown back, eyes mere slits, and her neck long and exposed. She turned Charlie on even more. Every bit of Ava sparked arousal in Charlie. The patrician line of her nose. The thought of her painted fingernails digging into Charlie's flesh. The syncopated sighs coming from her mouth. How her heels dug into the flesh just above Charlie's behind. They were one now. And Charlie reached that space where her body took over, where she was only feeling and sensation and fire. The fire came from somewhere deep inside her body, and was stoked every time Ava uttered another cry of pleasure. Charlie was right there with Ava.

Ava brought one hand to the back of Charlie's head and pulled her close, her mouth brushing Charlie's ear. "Oh, God, Charlie," Ava whispered. "Oh—" Then, along with her body, her voice stilled for a moment, her legs tightening around Charlie's middle, her nails digging into her skull.

Charlie gave one last thrust, delved deep inside Ava one last time. Her clit rubbed against the panel, which was now soaked in her wetness, and she cried out at the same time Ava did.

Ava's legs fell away, but her arms remained curled around Charlie's neck. Charlie fell against her, her body stunned by this orgasm. Hers and Ava's—but mostly hers. When she came to her senses, she remembered she was still inside Ava, and levered herself up again, looking down from Ava's face to between her legs. The sight of the dildo slipping from Ava's swollen lips ignited a new fire where the previous one had started. She understood now why Ava had woken her. Charlie, too, wanted to repeat variations of this all day long.

"Come here." Ava waved impatiently with her arm.

Charlie didn't bother taking the harness off and landed half on top of Ava.

"Did you come?" Ava asked, bringing her hands to Charlie's cheeks and positioning her face in front of hers.

"You know me. Easily combustible." Charlie grinned.

"Oh, Charlie." Ava craned her neck and planted a kiss on Charlie's lips. "That was so incredibly hot."

"Tell me about it."

"I think you deserve your breakfast now." Ava smiled one of those wide, toothy smiles. "You must keep up your strength. It's going to be a long day."

CHAPTER TWENTY-SIX

"Even I can get star struck," Ava said. "Elisa Fox belongs to the big league."

They were on their way to the wrap party of season one of *Underground*. All ten episodes had been filmed. A fact that excited Charlie disproportionately. Regardless, if a season two of the show was commissioned, Charlie wouldn't be part of the writing staff, making this party an even more emotional event for her.

"Are you okay?" Ava asked. She squeezed Charlie's leg.

"Yeah, just, I don't know… Coming to Hollywood and witnessing the birth of Underground the TV show has been quite the experience. It has exceeded my expectations in many ways, even though some of those ways were highly surprising." Charlie cast a glance at Ava, who, despite the brief to not dress up, looked über-glamorous in a tight, red dress and matching lipstick. Charlie suspected the presence of Elisa Fox had something to do with that. "I'm also nervous because I'm to give a speech, which is hardly my strong suit."

Ava curled her lips into a smile. "When you're giving the speech, focus on how wet you're making me just by standing there and being all gorgeous and cute… and mine."

"Oh, Christ, Ava." Charlie rolled her eyes. "That's not helping at all."

"Hm." Ava clutched her fingers around Charlie's

knee a little more tightly. "Let me try again." Her fingers loosened and started walking upward, in the direction of Charlie's crotch. "The advantage of living in Malibu is it takes long enough to get anywhere to take off the pressure." Ava's fingers had reached the apex of Charlie's upper thighs and remained there, stroking lightly. Charlie could barely feel anything through the fabric of her jeans, yet her clit responded to Ava's words and actions by swelling and pushing against the confines of her underwear.

"Again. Not helping." Charlie put her hand over Ava's between her legs, flattening it.

Ava sighed. "Okay then, let me try something else." She pulled her hand away and put it on Charlie's shoulder turning to face her as best she could in the backseat of a car. "Without you, this show would not exist. It came from your brain. You conceived of it. You wrote it, and then came to Hollywood to help shape it. You've done your part, whether you give a speech or not—and I'm sure no one will hold it against you if you don't. Your work speaks for itself. Besides, you're a writer. You can always use that as an excuse."

Warmth spread through Charlie's chest. "Hot, sweet, and wise," Charlie said. "How on earth did I end up with someone like you?"

"Definitely because I choose to only see the best in people." Ava's face was serious, but there was a smile in her voice.

Charlie chuckled, but quickly succumbed to nerves again. "It would be different if I didn't feel as though I also had to say a sort of goodbye."

"Then look at it differently. This is not goodbye. It's only the beginning. You'll have the premiere party in a few months. You'll have a few promotional activities to do. And if the show does get renewed, you will still be a part of it, even if you choose a more limited role. You'll always be a huge part of it."

"I guess." Charlie pursed her lips.

"I know you a bit by now, Charlie Cross. You're nervous because this whole journey has been so overwhelming for you, and this wrap party marks some sort of ending for you. I understand. And I'm with you every step of the way."

Charlie grabbed Ava's other hand, brought it to her mouth, and kissed it. "More than that, it marks a big transition for me. For the longest time, I believed that this was what I wanted. The glamour that comes with working on a TV show, with being on set as someone like Elisa Fox recites lines I came up with, to gaze up at the Hollywood sign and feel as though I belong. But I was wrong. All I want is to sit in a room by myself and make up more drama."

"Such is life." Ava cupped Charlie's jaw in her palm. "Everything is a process, and the process never ends. God knows where we'll be in a few years' time. Where life will take us."

Ava's use of the word "us" when talking about the future dislodged a knot in Charlie's stomach. It was Ava who made her feel as if she belonged. Ava, and Nick and Jason, and Liz and Sarah, and her softball team, and now even Jo. It was the people, not the place and its connotations and the gravity Charlie had awarded to it for years, that anchored her here.

The car slowed, and they pulled into the studio's parking lot.

"Everything's going to be all right, Charlie. I promise you," Ava said. If anyone else had spoken those words to her under any other circumstances, Charlie would have instantly cataloged them as bullshit, but coming from Ava, Charlie believed them.

* * *

Elisa Fox had brought her fellow A-list husband to the party, and the pair of them were the center of attention. Even though this was a private event, it was also the first time Charlie and Ava had stepped out together. Charlie had been beaming with pride since they'd arrived. She'd introduced Ava to Liz and her fellow writers, making her feel like part of a proper couple again.

"This has, by far, been the most amazing experience of my life," Liz said.

"Hey." Sarah elbowed her in the biceps.

"Apart from marrying my lovely wife, of course." Liz rubbed her upper arm as if Sarah's jab had actually hurt.

"How long have you been married?" Ava asked.

"Three years and a few weeks," Sarah said.

"Wow." Ava grinned at Liz and Sarah. "That must be—"

The sound of a piece of cutlery being tapped against a glass silenced them. "Ladies and gentlemen, may I have your attention, please?" It was Michelle, the showrunner. "Unfortunately, it is now time for the speeches." She pulled up her shoulders as if apologizing. "I know it's dreadful, but it needs to be done." The crowd laughed. Some even applauded. Charlie's stomach contracted in an unpleasant way. "I'll go first," Michelle said.

While she regaled the people around her with some anecdotes of the shoot, Ava moved behind Charlie and put a hand on her shoulder. "You'll be fine," she whispered in Charlie's ear. "I love you."

Ava's words connected with the ball of nerves in Charlie's stomach, and managed to undo some of it.

Michelle ended her speech with, "I'm going to keep it short, and I hope the people who will speak after me will do the same."

Even Elisa chuckled at that one.

Michelle turned toward Charlie. "Next, I will give the floor to the person without whom none of us would be here. Charlie Cross."

Ava's hand slid off Charlie's shoulder as she stepped forward. The venue for the party was a back room on the studio lot, with the lights dimmed and the tables shoved to the side. The only really glamorous attributes were the endless supply of champagne, the presence of Elisa and her husband. And, of course, Ava. There was no spotlight trained on Charlie, nor was there a stage she needed to step on. The casual nature reassured her somewhat. She waited for the mild applause to die down, and for Liz to stop whistling before starting to speak.

"I came up with this character a long time ago," Charlie started. "And to now stand here before all of you, knowing that within months Aretha will be a person of flesh and blood, so expertly embodied by the wonderful Elisa Fox, being broadcast into millions of people's living rooms," she shook her head gently, "is a bit of a strange feeling, I must admit." Charlie gave a nervous chuckle. "It has been a real honor and privilege to work with each and every one of you. You've taught me so much. When I first arrived here I didn't know much about how any of this TV making business worked, and it's been a dream come true. I've learned so much, made a few friends along the way—"

"And picked up Ava Castaneda," someone shouted from the side. It was Diana, the second camera woman.

"Yes, and there's that." Charlie refused to feel mortified about that. She looked to her right, to where Ava was standing. Ava gave her a big, comforting smile. "All in all, it has been an unforgettable experience. You've all been amazing to work with and… Thank you for making this girl's dream come true."

People started clapping. Charlie gave a quick, courteous bow, and headed back into the crowd. She didn't speak of how *Underground* had changed her in ways she would have never imagined. How, when she'd written the first pages of the first volume, not long after falling head over heels in love with Jo, in her tiny apartment in Greenwich Village, this outcome was the least likely one. But here she was, at a wrap party in a studio in Hollywood, about to listen to Elisa Fox's speech.

"I'm going to reward you for that," Ava whispered in her ear. Charlie hadn't said anything extraordinary or especially invigorating. She'd basically said what any contestant on *Knives Out* says once they're booted off. But Ava knew what it all really meant to her, and the two of them silently sharing that knowledge was more than enough for Charlie.

EPILOGUE

"Come on, I just put this on," Charlie said, but didn't make any moves to push Ava away.

"I don't care, Charlie. I want you so much right now, I might explode if I don't have you." Ava unbuttoned the shirt Charlie had just put on. It was freshly ironed for the big occasion: the book launch party of her first post-*Underground* novel *Release the Stars*, for which they would now probably be late.

Ava went to work on the button of Charlie's pants next. They were made of leather and clung so closely to Charlie's skin, she was worried about how long it would take to peel them off and then slip back into them again. But, apparently, Ava didn't need to see a lot of flesh. She just flipped open the button, undid the zipper, and regarded Charlie with lust filled eyes. She pushed Charlie's shirt slightly off her shoulders and plunged her hand inside Charlie's underpants.

When her finger dipped low enough to feel how wet Charlie was, Ava asked, "Was it the pants, Charlie? Does leather make you horny?"

"It's you," Charlie said between short bursts of breath. "Anything you do always drives me wild."

"I am so, so proud of you." Ava slipped her finger lower and, despite the limited wiggle room, managed to avoid grazing Charlie's clit. She went straight for Charlie's entrance. Her other hand rested on Charlie's neck, her thumb on her clavicle. "Besides, I know what you're like when you have to address an audience. Just taking off the pressure for you, baby." She flashed Charlie a smile, and let her finger go a little deeper, not slipping all the way in, but deep enough to cut off Charlie's breath for a split second.

Charlie pressed the flat of her hand to the wall for support. As Ava's finger found its way farther inside her, she thought of the dedication she'd included in her book. It was Ava herself who had said, "I think this one is for Jo more than for anyone else." By 'anyone else' she'd meant herself.

To Jo, the only one who could tell me what I needed to hear.

It was simple but clear. Charlie didn't know if she would be here, standing against a wall in Ava's house, where she'd as good as taken up residence, with one of Ava's fingers inside of her, coaxing her to a quick orgasm, if Jo hadn't set her straight that day.

Ava added another finger and, in the process, let her thumb drift along Charlie's clit. The nails of her other hand dug into the flesh of Charlie's neck in a wordless demand. It didn't take much for Charlie to meet it.

Ava's breath rushed over her face. Her eyes narrowed with every stroke she delivered. Ava deserved a dedication in *Release the Stars* just as much as Jo did. Starting to write again the way she had always done, had freed her. She'd been able to reconnect with all the feelings she'd stowed away, and poured them out through her fingers, onto her computer screen—and now onto the pages of the book. Charlie wasn't sure she could have done that for anyone other than Ava.

Sometimes, she'd come down from the room Ava had set up as an office for her—a temporary room at first that soon became Charlie's primary place to write—and sit with her laptop at the outside table where she and Ava had shared their first dinner. It had been an experiment at first. Charlie had been convinced she wouldn't be able to write a decent sentence with Ava so near, but Ava had insisted, claiming it would be excellent foreplay, so Charlie had, of course, given in. To her surprise, Ava's presence—as long as it was non-intrusive—didn't bother her. Instead, it made her tap the keys even faster, because she knew what that furious pace did to Ava.

"This is news to me, too," Ava had said, after she'd gotten up from the sun lounger she'd been relaxing on. "But the sound of you typing has made me incredibly wet."

"Come for me, Charlie." Ava was never the best at keeping her requests silent. She really did love the sound of her own voice. Charlie could hardly hold that against her. The pressure of her thumb grew more insistent, and that familiar quick rush of blood through her veins hit Charlie, that tingling sensation underneath her skin, that burst of joy emanating from where Ava's fingers worked inside her.

Charlie took a deep breath and sagged against the wall, while Ava let her hand slip from her pants. The skin of her wrist was red because of the friction with the leather, and Charlie brought it to her mouth and kissed it, smelling herself on Ava's fingers.

"You have no impulse control," Charlie said, in between pecks.

"Why on earth would I control myself when it comes to you?" Ava dug her knee between Charlie's legs.

Charlie didn't know what to say to that. Instead, she shook her head and chuckled. Then her eye caught the clock on the wall. "Shit. You'd better really let me get dressed now."

"Leave the top button of your blouse open," Ava said. "So I can dream a little when I look at you on stage."

* * *

The turn-out for Charlie's book launch was much bigger than anything she'd experienced before. Underground had started airing three weeks ago to great critical acclaim. Talks were already under way for season two, with a positive decision from the network deemed imminent.

"My favorite person on the planet," Estelle said. She was Charlie's LA agent, the one dealing with all things TV rights.

"You're only saying that because I made it rain for you," Charlie quipped. She hugged the tiny woman, and continued to work the room, Ava safely by her side. Charlie reveled in this moment. All her LA friends were here, and even a few select ones from New York had made the trip. Nick and Jason, in impeccable suits as usual, stood beaming in Elisa Fox's spotlight. Charlie had never exchanged that many words with the A-lister, and she doubted the actress had read anything else by her than *Underground*, but the network had considered it a good promotional idea to have Elisa make an appearance at Charlie's book launch. Charlie was glad it diverted some of the attention away from her.

For her, this was a celebration. A gathering with her nearest and dearest to acknowledge the birth of her new book and all the things it stood for. "Charlie Cross 2.0" Nick had called her a few weeks ago, at the premiere party for *Underground*, where he had also remained no more than three feet away from Elisa Fox at all times. "Not that different, just with a few necessary bug fixes," had been his exact words. Charlie had only been slightly offended.

"Congratulations, Charlie," Nick said, after finally extricating himself from underneath Elisa Fox's halo. "I can't wait to not read it." Nick only read magazines and TV scripts. Perhaps that was why he had become one of Charlie's closest friends. What she did professionally didn't matter to him. At the *Underground* premiere party he had also been caught saying, "So glad to finally be able to read one of your books, Charlie." Although he'd been the first to organize a viewing party every Sunday evening when a new episode was on.

Charlie accepted his embrace, and he pulled her a little closer than he normally would.

Behind them, Jo and Christian stood chatting with Liz and Sarah.

"The way you carried on, I believed your ex was a monster, and her boyfriend the embodiment of Satan on earth, but they're actually lovely people," Liz had said after Charlie had introduced them to each other. "You and your flair for the dramatic." What Charlie would miss most about the writers' room, were her chats with Liz during breaks and going for after-work drinks.

"Charlie." Christian extended his hand as usual. Charlie swatted it away and opened her arms for a hug.

"How very LA of you," he said to her when his mouth was closest to her ear.

"I didn't really mean it, you know," Jo said after they'd greeted each other. "You didn't really need to dedicate a book to me."

"I did." Charlie looked at Jo, at this woman who had changed her life—twice. Of course she didn't have to dedicate *Release the Stars* to her, but she had wanted to.

The next cluster of people consisted of Charlie's softball team members.

"Way to get off your high and mighty pedestal," Tiff joked. Now that most of Charlie's days were made up of writing and more writing, she'd had plenty of time to make every single game and training session of the season. Ava had even come along a few times to cheer her on from the sidelines and drink a few beers with the girls, but it hadn't influenced Charlie's batting average in a positive way at all.

Josie stood to the side of the circle, to Charlie's right. Charlie found her gaze and smiled. Josie smiled back and lifted her eyebrows, as if to repeat what she always said to Charlie when they saw each other, which was often now that Charlie was a team regular. "Don't forget. You owe me one most spectacular date."

Charlie bowed her head in acquiescence. Josie winked at her.

Behind Josie, in the furthest corner of the room, a tall grey figure skulked. Charlie turned to Ava. "Is that Eric?"

Ava craned her neck, which wasn't really necessary seeing as she towered over most people present. "Do they let any B-lister on the guest list here or what?" she said.

Eric and Ava's friendly relationship had cooled down considerably since Dallas. In the hiatus between seasons, Ava hadn't socialized with him at all—much to Charlie's relief.

Charlie glanced at Eric again. He had a copy of her book in his hands. When he noticed Charlie looking at him, he held up the book and made a signature gesture with his finger. *The nerve of this guy.* But Charlie wasn't in the mood to give him a piece of her mind. Eric could go fuck himself royally. He brought his hands together now, in a pleading gesture, and took a bow.

"You don't have to talk to him if you don't want to," Ava said. She'd started pre-production for the next season of *Knives Out* already, and had to deal with Eric in a professional setting. "I'll go. You should enjoy your evening."

Charlie appreciated Ava's protective instinct, but she'd sign Eric's book if that was what he wanted. She knew just what to write.

"It's okay." Charlie pressed her way through the crowd swiftly, until she stood face-to-face with the man who had found her biggest weakness and shamelessly exploited it in Dallas.

"Charlie." He paused. "I won't stand here in front of you and pretend an apology can ever be enough. I know it can't. Nevertheless, I would like to tell you how sorry I am for the things I said. Obviously, none of it was true. I was jealous and being an asshole. I'm old enough to know when I'm wrong and out of line." He shuffled his weight around a bit. "Oh, and by the way, *Underground* is my new favorite show. Best thing on TV in ages." He glanced at Ava. "Apart from our show, of course." The smile he gave them appeared genuine enough.

"I'll sign your book," Charlie said and held out her hand.

Eric handed it to her. Charlie took it and a pen from her blazer's front pocket, and signed it. *Charlie Cross, Ava Castaneda's lesbian lover.*

She gave the book back to Eric. "Enjoy."

Eric read her inscription and grinned. "Good one. Thanks."

The sound of a finger tapping on a microphone relieved Charlie of having to engage in conversation with Eric much longer.

"Looks like things are about to kick off," Eric said. "Thanks again, Charlie. I'll leave you to it." Just like that, he disappeared into the crowd.

Charlie didn't have time to discuss this encounter with Ava, because Andrew, her publisher, had taken the stage. A word of warning would have been nice, she thought, as she made her way to him.

"Charlie? Charlotte Cross? Where are you?" Andrew said, casting his gaze over the crowd. "Ah, magnificent." He'd located Charlie, who was making her way to the podium. "Welcome, distinguished guests and Charlie Cross readers. Charlie will say a few words now, and perhaps do us the honor of reading a few pages from her new masterpiece, after which there will be a signing session. Drinks will be available aplenty throughout. Enjoy."

"Go kick some ass, baby," Ava said. Charlie turned around and kissed Ava on the mouth before taking the stage.

"Hello all," she said. A spotlight blinded her—just like it had done the night of the auction. "Let me tell you a few things about how this book came about." Charlie cleared her throat and started at the beginning.

ACKNOWLEDGEMENTS

Endless gratitude to you, my reader, without whom I wouldn't be living my dream of waking up every day to write more stories. To my wife, whose crazy idea I once was. To my editor Jove Belle whose knowledge, skill and tough love made this book a much better read. To my Launch Team for the boundless enthusiasm and loyalty.

Thank you.

ABOUT THE AUTHOR

Harper Bliss is the author of the novels *Once in a Lifetime* and *At the Water's Edge*, the *High Rise* series, the *French Kissing* serial and several other lesbian erotica and romance titles. She is the co-founder of Ladylit Publishing, an independent press focusing on lesbian fiction. Harper lives on an outlying island in Hong Kong with her wife and, regrettably, zero pets.

Harper loves hearing from readers and if you'd like to drop her a note you can do so via harperbliss@gmail.com

Website: www.harperbliss.com
Facebook: facebook.com/HarperBliss
YouTube: youtube.com/c/HarperBliss

15346462R00138

Printed in Great Britain
by Amazon